"You have no idea how irresistible you are."

"I'm afraid I lack town polish, James."

He touched the curve of her cheek, which glowed in the moonlight. "Any gem may be polished. It is the quality that interests me," he murmured. "I've wanted to do this ever since I saw you at the inn," he said, and pulled her into his arms to kiss her.

The kiss blended perfectly with the night and the stars. It was like another gift of nature. The first strangeness soon passed, and she felt at ease in his arms, despite the excitement that raced in her blood. No thought of the thousands of acres of his estate or of the London mansion occurred to her. She only knew she had magically found the man who was made for her, and she reveled in his love.

Also by Joan Smith
Published by Fawcett Books:

BABE
AURORA
LACE FOR MILADY
VALERIE
THE BLUE DIAMOND
REPRISE
WILES OF A STRANGER
LOVER'S VOWS
RELUCTANT BRIDE
LADY MADELINE'S FOLLY
LOVE BADE ME WELCOME
MIDNIGHT MASQUERADE
ROYAL REVELS
THE DEVIOUS DUCHESS
TRUE LADY
BATH BELLES
STRANGE CAPERS
A COUNTRY WOOING
LOVE'S HARBINGER
LETTERS TO A LADY
COUNTRY FLIRT
LARCENOUS LADY
MEMOIRS OF A HOYDEN

SILKEN SECRETS

Joan Smith

FAWCETT CREST • NEW YORK

A Fawcett Crest Book
Published by Ballantine Books
Copyright © 1988 by Joan Smith

Library of Congress Catalog Card Number: 87-92133

ISBN 0-449-21372-2

Manufactured in the United States of America

First Edition: August 1988

Chapter One

Respectable families usually confine their skeletons to a closet. Lord Exholme found his own closet too close for comfort and packed his younger brother, Lord Edwin Horton, off to the next county. Horton Hall, on the marshy coast of Kent, was a crumbling heap owned by an uncle. There was no doing anything with such a small property, and there was no doing anything with Lord Eddie. He had failed at university. He had failed to catch the boat arranged to take him to India to make his fortune. He had made a shambles of his sojourn at the Admiralty and topped this illustrious career not only by marrying a penniless woman but adopting the woman's niece when her own parents died. Generosity was considered quite another vice by Lord Exholme, who refused to have anything to do with either his brother or the young girl. This arrangement suited all three right down to their toes.

It was the middle of the night when Lord Edwin was awakened from a deep sleep by the gentle drip, drip of rain coming through the ceiling. He opened a bleary eye and cursed. Why did roofs have to go leaking on a man's head? A lead roof was supposed to last for a hundred years. Just his luck that the century since the last reroofing of Horton Hall should fall during his tenure. Let it rain!

He pulled the blanket over his head and tried in vain to recapture oblivion. A shower in his bedchamber meant the attics were awash. As if to confirm this lugubrious thought, the patter of mice's feet above told him his unwanted tenants were scampering for high ground.

He stuck his head beneath the pillow. There, that was a little better. No sooner did he begin to feel the gentle lassitude of sleep creep over him than there was a racket at his door and Fitch came pelting in.

"Here, Lord Eddie!" his servant rasped. "A lugger's run aground right in your bay."

Lord Edwin pulled his head from beneath the pillow and sat up. "Go away, Fitch!" he said, in what he imagined to be a stern way. His querulous, whining voice was incapable of sternness. It grated on the sensitive ear like a slate pencil. "It's the middle of the night. How is a man supposed to get any sleep, between torrents of rain and herds of mice and footmen hollering at the top of their lungs!"

"I ain't a footman!" Fitch reminded his employer. "You promoted me to butler when you couldn't afford to pay my wages last quarter." Fitch frequently received promotions in lieu of salary. At his present rate of ascent, he'd soon be master of the Hall.

"So I did. So I did. Sorry, Fitch, but please go away."

Lord Edwin lay back down and pulled the pillow over his head. Fitch was wise in the ways of his master and stood waiting. In about sixty seconds the grizzled head rose again from the bed. "A lugger, you say?"

"Aye, sitting aground, just waiting to be relieved of her cargo."

Lord Edwin jumped out of bed and stood grinning. Had he been visible in the dark, he would have been a comical sight. A pair of dark blue eyes, too close together for beauty, were dancing with delight. He wore a handker-

2

chief knotted over his head and a flannelette nightshirt down to his knobby knees. Below this, a pair of spindly white legs stood, bowed to a nearly perfect circle.

Fitch struck a flint and lit a tallow candle. Every economy was practiced at Horton Hall, unless a luxury could be purchased on tick. The stores in the village had become rather testy about supplying more beeswax candles until the last three years' worth had been paid for. Neither man took any notice of the disheveled room that sprang into view. There are some things best ignored, and the state of Horton Hall was one of those things.

"You think they might give us a barrel if we let them store it here?" Lord Edwin asked hopefully. "The customs men will be after them before morning."

"They've left the ship," Fitch told him.

"Left the ship? Then they've already unloaded," he said, and sat down with a sigh. He could almost taste the brandy. Excellent strong stuff they got here on the coast, before it was hauled off to London and destroyed with water and caramel sugar.

"Nay," Fitch assured him with a gurgle of pure joy. "They hadn't time. They went astray in the storm and landed here in your way instead of at Vulch's dredged dock. With the excisemen hot on their tails, they leapt overboard and ran for cover to avoid capture."

"Egad! Then we have a parcel of vicious Frenchies hiding nearby. The doors, Fitch! Secure the doors!"

"The devil with the doors! Get into your trousers, and we'll have a barrel off the lugger before they come back."

Lord Edwin sat rubbing his chin nervously. He would like a barrel of that brandy—yet did he want it enough to risk the wrath of the French smugglers?

"They wouldn't have stayed this close to the boat," Fitch said. "They'd canter along toward Vulch's place.

3

He'd be sure to hide 'em and get them back safely to France.''

It was no secret in the community that Mr. Adrian Vulch was the gentleman in charge of smuggling at the English end. This in no way detracted from his excellent reputation as the chief man of business in Dymchurch. Quite the contrary. He was a large employer and paid better than an honest man could afford. He was a Member of Parliament and held several other prestigious positions, including warden of the church.

The knotted handkerchief bobbed in decision. ''We'll go for it, Fitch,'' Lord Edwin decided, and began scrambling into his buckskins. ''Prepare the ship.''

''Mind you hurry down and give me a hand, and don't go nodding off again,'' Fitch said, and loped out the door.

It was not only a lack of wages that caused the ''butler'' to take such a high hand with his master. Fitch had come to Lord Edwin ten years before on the understanding that he was to be trained up as a bruiser. Even at fifteen years, Fitch had had the build of an ox. ''A cross between a bull and Adonis'' was the housekeeper's description of him, for Fitch was handsome as well as big and strong. Of course, the promise was yet to be kept.

The vessel used to reach the grounded lugger was no ship but Fitch's flat-bottomed fishing boat. When Fitch wasn't busy being the groom, butler, and sole footman at Horton Hall, he was the cook's helper. His help usually consisted of catching seafood for dinner.

When Lord Edwin had dressed and gone to the shore, Fitch took up the oars and began plying them. With his massive shoulders and arms like legs, he skimmed the heavy boat through the reeds as easily as he breathed.

Lord Edwin sat huddled in a blanket while Fitch rowed them in the rain across the black water to the lugger. Once they had reached the ship, Fitch clambered aboard and had to lift Lord Edwin up, for that ineffectual gentleman hadn't a notion of how to climb. They soon stood on deck, looking into dark corners for their prize.

"There are no barrels here, Fitch," Lord Edwin pointed out. "You've brought me on a fool's errand. Brandy, indeed!"

"She'd be below deck," Fitch told him.

"Below deck, eh? And how would a fellow get below deck? I don't see a staircase."

"There'd be a hole and a ladder," Fitch said.

"That sounds very inconvenient. Holes and ladders. Just what you'd expect of the French."

"Here it is," Fitch said, and disappeared below.

Lord Edwin went down after him, grumbling, "We need a light, Fitch. But I'll tell you something; there's no brandy here. I can't smell it."

Fitch felt around and found a flint box. He lit a rush lamp and held it high. "You're right," he said. "There's no brandy."

"My throat craves brandy. The sweet sting of it, the needles on the tongue. Why did you get me all excited, Fitch? That's a cruel stunt to play on an old man who's just made you his butler."

Fitch looked at the strange bales piled in the hold and began ripping at the papers of one.

"You're wasting your time. It ain't brandy," his master said. "Brandy comes in barrels." After a moment he was curious enough to go and see just what it was that occupied Fitch. "It's cloth," he said.

"Aye, silk," Fitch agreed.

He unrolled the end of one bolt and held up a length of shimmering golden silk. "Very fine silk," he said in a meaningful way. He continued unrolling till he had measured one piece. "About ten ells, it looks like. There must be a hundred bales here."

"What good is silk? You can't drink it."

"You can *sell* it," Fitch said, and waited for light to penetrate the murky corners of his master's mind.

"Sell it? But it's not ours. Oh, you mean . . . Yes, I see." When he was occupied in larcenous thought, Lord Edwin's fingers played along his cheek, tapping nervously. He nodded his head. His close-set eyes gleamed with greed, giving him something of the air of a hungry ferret. "A fair bit of it here, Fitch."

"Easier to steal and hide than brandy," Fitch pointed out.

"Well, let us get on with it."

The "us" was rhetorical. Lord Edwin's contribution was to hold the rush lamp while Fitch struggled up the ladder with the bales and placed them one by one in his boat. He had to make two trips to shore, but after a while, one hundred bolts of finest silk, each containing ten ells, sat on the shore, and not a soul knew it but Fitch and Lord Edwin. The next problem was where to store it. The excisemen would be out scouring the coast for it by morning. More dangerous, the Frenchies would be after it, and possibly Vulch's men as well.

Fitch was gasping from his exertions, but he knew he couldn't leave the silk there. "Where do you want it?" he asked.

"Put it some place safe, Fitch. I'm for bed. It's hard work, moving all those bales." He stretched and imagined an ache in his unused muscles.

"The attic?"

"Attic—ho, you're mad, my good man. The attics are awash. Any corner that isn't flooded is overrun with hungry mice."

"The cellars, then?"

"That's the first place they'll look. No, I don't want it in the house. We'll leave it outdoors, but well hidden. If

6

it's found, they'll never be able to prove we took it. But hide it well, Fitch. It would be a pity to lose it after all my work.''

"But where?'' Fitch persisted.

"Good grief, do I have to do everything? Hide it in the hay wain.''

As he spoke, Lord Edwin nodded at a derelict hay wagon that had stood for decades, listing to the left where one wheel was lost. What it had ever been doing so close to shore was a mystery to him. Some misguided soul must have had a picnic here. Wretched things, with sand in your food and the stench of seaweed. People had some very peculiar ideas of entertainment.

His duty done, Lord Edwin straggled back to the Hall and sat waiting for Fitch. He took the clever idea of not having any lamps on, in case the Frenchies were snooping around outside, and nearly frightened Fitch out of his boots when he came in an hour later.

"It took you long enough!'' he griped.

Fitch was panting. "I had to take the hay out of the wagon and put the bales inside, then cover them up again, making sure to get dry hay on the bottom. I put the extra hay under the wagon. That old wain's been there forever. No one will think of looking there for the silk.''

"It was a good idea. *My* idea,'' he reminded his helper. "I've been doing some ciphering, Fitch. I figure I made something in the neighborhood of a thousand pounds tonight. One hundred bales, at ten ells a bale. That's a thousand ells. And Bertie tells me I have no head for figures. Ha! It would sell for somewhere in the neighborhood of a pound or guinea an ell, I believe. Don't think I don't appreciate your help. I'll manage a little something toward your back wages out of this haul.''

Fitch smiled to hear it.

"What's that you've got there?" Lord Edwin asked, as he spotted something in his servant's hands.

"It's a shawl," Fitch said. "It was in one of the bales. I thought I might give it to Miss Judson for her birthday tomorrow."

"Is it Mary Anne's birthday again tomorrow?" Lord Edwin asked peevishly. Bother! That meant he should buy her a present. He rather thought he'd forgotten to the last few years. A young girl should get a present for her birthday. "Bring it up to my room and let's get a look at it."

They went upstairs, and Lord Edwin laid the shawl on his counterpane. It was a gold triangle of silk, with three ends heavily embroidered in various hues. "This is beautiful," he said. "All worked by hand. Look at that pattern—flowers and birds and bees. A trifle risqué, that. But Mary Anne is too young to be aware of such carrying-on."

Fitch started to hear a young lady of twenty-four was too young for anything. "Nay, Lord Eddie. She's getting on."

"Is she, by God? Yes, I suppose she is. *Tempus fugit*, Fitch. That's Latin. Old fugitive time. A nice fringe," he said, fingering the threads. "Mary Anne will love it. Thank you, Fitch."

Fitch blinked. "You're welcome."

"Were there any more of these embroidered pieces?"

"Not in the bales I opened. It was all just straight material."

"Odd they should put one finished piece in. I expect it's a sample, to show what can be done. Yes, very nice."

"When will we be moving the silk?" Fitch asked.

"The sooner we get rid of it, the better. I can't unload it in Dymchurch. I'll have to ride over to Folkestone. I'll stop at a few drapery shops there tomorrow and see what kind of deal I can arrange. It will be best not to actually

8

move it till things settle down here in a day or so. You must keep an eye on the hay wain, Fitch. Don't let anyone near it. And you'd best go up to the attic tomorrow and mop up the flood, too.''

''How can I guard the hay wain, then?''

''You'll think of something. I daresay you can see it from the attic and go rushing down if anyone comes around. Now, I'm for bed. I wish it had been brandy,'' he said sadly, and sat down to allow Fitch to remove his boots.

Sleep didn't come immediately. Lord Edwin still maintained some vestige of a conscience, but it was fear of yet another dismal failure that kept him awake. His past was littered with failures, every one of them Bertie, his older brother, was only too eager to throw in his face. ''You must start at the bottom, Eddie,'' he always said. How the deuce should the son of an earl, born at the top of a hill, know what folks did ''at the bottom''? Perhaps this was it—they stole. There couldn't be anything much lower than stealing. Yet, outwitting the Frenchies was hardly stealing. No, no, it was an Englishman's duty. Success was his duty, too, but Lord Edwin was prey to a dreadful foreboding tnat success would once again elude him.

Chapter Two

The first thing Mary Anne Judson noticed when she opened her eyes the next morning was that the sun was shining. Tiny golden rays filtered through the lacy leaves of the black walnut tree beyond her window. They pierced the room with shafts of magic, like fairy wands. Then she remembered it was the first of May—her birthday—and a little feeling of excitement curled in her breast. Twenty-four years ago today she had been born to the woman whose picture sat on her dresser beside the miniature of Uncle Edwin. The picture was really the only means she had of recalling her mother. She felt sad that she couldn't remember more, but she mustn't get to feeling sorry for herself on this special day. After all, she had Uncle Edwin.

She smiled fondly as she thought of him. To the world he was a foolish wastrel, but to her he would always maintain some trace of the hero who had rescued her from the parish home for foundlings after her mother died. She had been only four years old at the time, but the nightmare still came occasionally to darken her dreams. She remembered standing right there by the beadle and Miss Monroe in the office at the parish home while they discussed her fate as though she were a stick of wood with no ears and no feelings. The office was a dreary green, with a plain wooden floor, the narrow planks turning up at the edges. Miss Monroe had worn a matron's white apron over her blue gown.

It had been late autumn, just the dreariest time of the year. Her papa's relatives had come for the funeral, but they were not close relatives. With children of their own to raise, they none of them wanted to be saddled with another. So, it was the parish home for her, and sleeping in the monkish dormitory surrounded by strange children, many of them older than she, all of them terrifying to a newly orphaned child.

It was only to be for a few weeks till her mama's relatives could be contacted. "They didn't even answer my letter. I never heard of such a thing," old Miss Monroe scolded to the beadle that morning. "Her mama was supposed to be so well connected—her sister married to a lord. Ha! *I* never believed it. It's obvious no one wants her. We'll have to keep her here, I suppose. Another mouth to feed. And look at her—ugly as sin. No hope of anyone taking her off our hands."

She hadn't really been ugly. It was the week of crying that had left her eyes swollen and red and her face shrunken in terror. Her hair, too, was unkempt, and the orphan gowns were horrid worsted things.

Then, while a helpless four-year-old child contemplated a life locked up in this prison with strangers, Uncle Edwin had come pouncing into the room.

"Where is she?" he demanded. "Where is my niece, Mary Anne Judson?"

Mary Anne had looked at him with her big brown eyes pooled with tears. He didn't look comical to her. Not then, not now. Never. He was her Sir Galahad.

"You're looking at her. And who might you be, sir?" Miss Monroe demanded.

11

Uncle had drawn himself up to his full five feet six inches and announced in that supercilious way he still used occasionally, "You are speaking to Lord Edwin Horton of Horton Hall in Kent, madam. Brother to the Earl of Exholme. I have come to fetch my niece home."

Then he had unstiffened and come toward her, holding a pretty doll. That was thoughtful of him, to bring a doll. "So this is Mary Anne. A pretty little thing, ain't she? Takes after her mama. The Beatons all had those lovely brown eyes, my own wife included."

It was like balm to her bruised spirit. She loved him on the spot, and she had no occasion ever to think her love was misplaced, even if he did sometimes forget her birthday. What did a present matter? He had given her a home and himself for a family.

She shook the thought away. May the first. Anything might happen on a girl's birthday, and to be ready for this nebulous possibility of pleasure, Mary Anne decided to wear her good sprigged muslin. She splashed cold water on her face and shivered into the pretty rose-sprigged gown. It was really too cold for muslin yet, but with that sun shining, it would soon warm up. She brushed her chestnut curls back from her face and caught them in a basket with the nacre comb Uncle had given her three birthdays ago. Last year and the year before he had forgotten her birthday, but perhaps this year he'd remember.

She rubbed her cheeks to give them a blush of color and examined her face in the mirror. Twenty-four years old! My, she was getting on. She really didn't look much different from last year. Her brown eyes sparkled as brightly. Her cheeks were still full. The simple country life held at bay the ravages of time, but one of these years she'd have to start rouging. Then the hair would silver, and soon her life would be over, before it had properly begun. Oh, dear, and she had felt so happy when she awoke.

Mary Anne wrapped a white wool shawl around her shoulders and went downstairs quietly to avoid waking Uncle Edwin. She suspected he found the days plenty long enough when he arose at ten or eleven. Horton Hall had no large acres to oversee, no tenant farmers, no forests, and no crops except the home garden and a few acres of hay for the horses and cow and the goat. Except that Belle, the goat, seemed to prefer eating the stalls and buckets and her rope. Belle's presence at the Hall was due to another of Lord Edwin's generous impulses. Mrs. Christian, their neighbor, had threatened to put the animal down when Belle ate her best umbrella. Uncle Edwin had retrieved the horrid goat from the axe, much to his housekeeper's dismay.

"There's all kinds of creatures in the world, and your uncle's one of them," she had told Mary Anne. "He means well, but he don't think what he's about."

Mrs. Plummer took care of the chickens, and Fitch did the outside work. Poor Uncle Edwin just got in his days as best he could. He'd probably get up at eleven and drive the gig into Dymchurch to talk to his cronies. She'd go with him today, to celebrate her birthday.

"Good morning, Mrs. Plummer," Mary Anne said brightly when she entered the breakfast room.

Mrs. Plummer's dour face creased in an unusual smile. Like Mary Anne, she had attempted to honor the day by dressing up. A new apron covered her dark gown, and her brindled hair was skimmed back even more tightly than usual from her rosy face. Poor tyke, she thought—it would be a day like any other for Miss Judson, but she'd do what she could. Fitch had orders to kill a chicken for dinner, and a raisin cake was in the process of being made in the kitchen.

"Happy birthday, Miss Judson. My, don't you look

pretty! Wearing your good gown, eh? I expect you'll be going into the village.''

"Perhaps," Mary Anne said evasively. If Uncle forgot it was her birthday, he might not invite her, and one hated to be the object of pity. "Just toast and tea for me, please."

Mary Anne saw the little vase of flowers on the table and smiled her thanks at this token of celebration. Already the loosestrife flowers were falling, sitting like golden stars on the table. While Mrs. Plummer poured the tea, she took a look out the bay window that gave a view of the water beyond. "Did the storm keep you awake last night?" she asked Miss Judson.

"Storm? I didn't even know it had rained." Mary Anne looked out the window and saw the French lugger. "Oh, dear, someone is shipwrecked right on our doorstep!" she exclaimed, and ran to the window for a closer look. It was an unusual-looking vessel. Its hull was low and broad. It had three masts, but the sails had been lowered. "It's not one of Vulch's ships," she said, frowning.

"They do say it's a French smuggling boat," Mrs. Plummer told her with a wise nod of her head. "Meg Castle stopped by on her way to Vulch's this morning, and they say in the village it got grounded on our sandbar in the storm. They didn't catch the Frenchies," she added.

Mary Anne's eyes grew wilder. "Then they're still around somewhere!"

The ladies exchanged a frightened glance. "I sharpened up my butcher knife. If the brutes come into my kitchen, they'll live to regret it," Mrs. Plummer said.

She went to make the toast, and Mary Anne stood looking out at the lugger. It must have gotten blown badly off its course. It was parallel with the shore, its bow riding a little higher than its stern. There would be some excitement today, with the excisemen seizing the cargo and tugboats pulling the lugger free. Uncle wouldn't want to miss that. Mary Anne mentally weighed the merits of going to Dymchurch versus staying home and watching Dymchurch come to them. Half the town would be here for the excitement.

When Mrs. Plummer returned with the toast, Mary Anne said, "I'm surprised Officer Codey isn't here, keeping an eye on the cargo."

"There isn't any cargo," Mrs. Plummer informed her. "Codey was here at five-thirty this morning. He had Fitch take him out in his boat, and the hold is empty as my cupboards. The Frenchies must have delivered before they got stuck."

"Oh. In that case, there won't be any hurry in removing the boat." Nor would Dymchurch come in mass for such paltry entertainment.

Mrs. Plummer placed the toast in front of Mary Anne. On the plate beside it there sat a little square box wrapped in silver paper. "Mrs. Plummer! You shouldn't have." Mary Anne smiled and eagerly pulled off the paper. "A diary! How lovely! I'll start writing it up right today. I've often wanted one. Thank you."

"I'm glad you like it." The dame smiled and returned to her kitchen. Just what you'll have to write in it is a mystery to me, my dear, she added to herself. A shame for a pretty lady like Miss Judson to wither on the vine. She would have liked to buy her something more, but with no wages for several months, a person was limited to the treasures already in her possession. It was a rare stroke of luck she'd won the diary at the church bazaar.

While Mrs. Plummer fretted and worried about her mistress, Miss Judson fondled the little leather diary and felt she was blessed to have such good friends. There were plenty of girls with no family and no friends—ladies, gently born like herself, who had to go out and work for a living as governess or nursemaid. She had Uncle Edwin and Mrs. Plummer, Fitch, and all the neighbors. She could probably have Joseph Horton, too, if she wanted him.

Her mind wandered to this neighbor and relative of Uncle Edwin. Joseph lived at Seaview, just a few miles down the coast. He was really a very nice gentleman, and it was a pity she couldn't care for him as she should. He was to inherit Horton Hall when Uncle Edwin died. Added to his own Seaview, he would be quite an eligible parti. He wasn't particularly ugly or ill-natured. "A long, dry drink of water" was Mrs. Plummer's peculiar description of Joseph. He had a good character, worked hard, went to church on Sundays, didn't drink to excess or gamble. Why couldn't she like him? Was it because of his slurs on Uncle Edwin? Was it the proprietary way he came to the Hall every week, condemning everything and often dropping a hint that the owner of an entailed estate could be forced by law to attend to its maintenance?

This certainly didn't do his suit any good, but even without that annoyance, Mary Anne knew she could never like Joseph Horton, much less love him. There was no romance in him. She dropped the crusts of toast on her plate and stared with unseeing eyes at the bay window. She probably had read too many novels. What she would like to write up in her new diary was that she had met an exciting new man—tall, dark, dashing. Maybe someone like the French smugglers. Someone who led a life of danger and intrigue . . .

"Good morning, my dear! Happy birthday!"

Mary Anne looked to the doorway and blinked in surprise. "Uncle, it's only eight o'clock! What are you doing up so early?"

And in his good jacket, too, she noticed. He's going somewhere—oh, I hope he takes me with him! Lord Edwin's dark eyes sparkled with mischief. She could see he was in an excellent mood, which was very strange. He didn't usually sleep when it rained, and lack of sleep turned him into a regular bear.

"We must celebrate your birthday, my dear. I thought we might drive you over to Folkestone and buy you a present. It isn't every day a young lady turns, er—eighteen, is it?"

"I'm twenty-four today, Uncle," she reminded him.

"Good God, you're becoming ancient! Twenty-four, eh? So much the better. Soon you can put on your caps and have done with all the wretched matchmaking business." It was really only Joseph Horton's attentions that brought on this testy speech. "Where is Plummer? I want gammon and eggs."

Uncle never had anything but toast and tea for breakfast. Often only tea. "Have you had some good news?" Mary Anne asked hopefully. "Did the government give you your pension?"

For twenty years Lord Edwin had been angling to get himself on the list of king's pensioners. Whitehall was proving remarkably stubborn about rewarding him for his five months of sitting at that demmed desk, with only one window in his office.

"Nothing of the sort. It is all Bertie's doings, keeping it from me. Ah, there she is. Gammon and eggs, Plummer."

"There's no gammon, Lord Edwin."

"No gammon? What kind of a house is this? You're twenty-four now, Mary Anne. Time you took hold of the reins and brought this place to order. Bring me some eggs, then—half a dozen eggs—and fry them in bacon fat. Don't tell me we have no bacon fat."

"We have plenty of that, and precious little else," Mrs. Plummer said, and strode from the room.

While Uncle was waiting for his breakfast to arrive,

17

Mary Anne told him about the grounded boat in the bay. He went to the window to view it but expressed no intention of staying home to watch it being hauled away. "Mrs. Plummer said the brandy had already been unloaded," Mary Anne mentioned.

"Brandy?" he asked, with a sharp look. Then he remembered to be ignorant on the subject. "All gone, eh? Too bad."

When he had eaten and Mary Anne had gone upstairs for her bonnet, Lord Edwin went in search of Fitch. He found him in the attic, floating beetles in the puddles. "I told you to keep an eye on the hay wain!" he exclaimed.

"Best not to stick too close to it. It might look suspicious," Fitch replied. "Codey's been and gone. I took him out to the boat myself. He's spending the day spying on Vulch's place, trying to catch the Frenchies."

"Ho, he underestimates his man if he thinks Vulch is stupid enough to let them get caught. They're long gone back to France. I've found an excellent excuse to go to Folkestone to make my inquiries."

"Who'll drive the carriage for you?"

"Damme, I'll have to borrow Jem from Mr. Christian. Scoot over and get him, Fitch. I'm taking Mary Anne for a birthday treat. I'll go to two or three draper shops and see where I can get the best price for the silk. You wrap up the shawl while I'm gone. I'll give it to her tonight and say I bought it in Folkestone."

"You'll have to keep her out of the way when you make your inquiries, then."

"A good point, Fitch. I'll tell her to choose some ribbons—that'll keep her busy." He rattled the coins in his pocket and pulled them out. A pitifully thin purse, but a lunch and ribbons could be eked out of it. In a week's time he'd have a thousand pounds, or possibly guineas.

18

"Carry on," he said, and returned below stairs to wait for Jem.

The drive along the coast to Folkestone was pretty in May, with all the greenery freshly washed by the storm the night before. The sea was an iridescent gold today, and the vessels on it rode as peacefully as toy boats. The ships' sails billowed, but they didn't bulge. On days like this Lord Edwin often wished he were a sailor, but he didn't speak the language. He never could tell what the admirals were talking about. Luffing and bows and spits—it was worse than Latin.

At Folkestone they took a spin along the leas at the top of the sea cliff before driving down to the picturesque old fishing town with its irregular streets. "Ah, here is a drapery shop," Lord Edwin exclaimed, and held the door for Mary Anne to enter. She had no idea what her present was to be. She suspected a length of material for a gown was beyond her uncle's purse, but doubted he had brought her all the way to Folkestone for ribbons, which was what he suggested she look at.

He was obviously planning to surprise her. She noticed across the shop that he asked for the manager and was shown into an office. Her curiosity mounted higher. Even a length of material hardly required a private conference. Then she smiled ruefully. Of course, Uncle wouldn't know that. She waited for the door to open and an impatient manager to show Uncle Edwin out. For ten minutes she waited, and when finally he emerged, the manager was smiling broadly. How very curious!

More curious still, Uncle didn't carry any parcel from the shop, but went across the road and repeated his performance in two other shops. It was the noon hour by the time they had canvassed all of the drapery stores, and they went back to the leas, still without a parcel, to have luncheon at Bates Hotel.

Lord Edwin was in fine fettle, praising the good merchants of Folkestone and their wares, laughing, and insisting she have a second glass of wine, but what he didn't mention was her gift. After luncheon he was still chirping merry and asked Mary Anne what she would like to do. Bereft of inspiration, she suggested they take a walk along the shrub-grown and sheltered paths between the leas and the Lower Sandgate Road. Knowing her uncle's aversion to churches, she only glanced at the Church of Saints Mary and Eanswith from outside, then returned to the carriage, and eventually they drove to Dymchurch, with pauses at Sandgate and Hythe to look in at a few more drapery shops. Lord Edwin's indifferent team was in no hurry to get home.

Chapter Three

It was just coming on evening when they entered Dymchurch. "We'll top off our outing with dinner at the inn," Lord Edwin announced. His pockets were to let by this time, but he had settled up at the inn last quarter day, and his credit was good there.

"I expect Mrs. Plummer has dinner waiting, Uncle," Mary Anne pointed out. It went against the grain to do it. Dinner at the inn was a rare treat, and on May Day there was bound to be a good crowd. The old traditional May Day celebrations had diminished, but the season still put folks in a holiday mood.

"Let it wait. We'll have it for a midnight snack," he said grandly, and pulled the check string.

He held the door, and Mary Anne went into the quaint little inn, which was bustling with unusual activity. "A private parlor, if you please," Lord Edwin ordered.

There was, of course, none to be found on this busy day. In fact, there was a small crowd waiting for a parlor. The talk was all about the grounded smuggling vessel. Word had gotten about that the cargo was silk, not brandy. Lord Edwin was impatient for his mutton and began to make a commotion with the inn servants. His annoyance rose to indignation when a parlor was freed and a Mr. Robertson was called to take possession of it.

"Now, see here!" he exclaimed. "I've been waiting the better part of an hour."

Mary Anne pulled at his elbow. "Only five minutes, Uncle," she whispered.

Lord Edwin knew Mr. Robertson was no inhabitant of Dymchurch and forged on to strengthen his spurious claim to the private parlor. "If you want to turn off a regular patron for a stranger, so be it," he said grandly. But to ensure that this inequity didn't occur, he added, "And call the proprietor while you're about it, my lad."

Meanwhile, Mr. Robertson had stepped out from the crowd and turned a disgruntled gaze on Lord Edwin. Mary Anne saw him, realized he was the challenger for the parlor, and felt a deep stab of regret that her uncle should be making a cake of himself in front of such an out-and-outer. Her breath stopped in her throat as she gazed. She had never seen such an attractive man in Dymchurch before. He might have stepped straight off a London stage. He had that dramatic, larger-than-life quality.

Yet, as she measured him, she decided he wasn't actually taller than six feet. Joseph was six feet two, but Joseph shrunk to insignificance beside this gentleman. Everything about the stranger was top of the trees. His dark hair, not quite black—it had coppery lights under the lamps—was meticulously barbered. It was brushed forward in the fashionable Brutus do. His profile, as he spoke to the clerk, was clean-cut. He had a sculptured nose and a granite-strong jaw. The eyes looked as black as thorn buds, and the overall contours of the face were extremely pleasing. He still wore afternoon clothes, but their London patina put the evening clothes of Dymchurch in the shade. A blue superfine jacket adhered to his body as closely as a second skin. A discreetly flowered waistcoat, an immaculate cravat, biscuit trousers, and shining Hessians completed his attire.

"Is there some problem?" the stranger said to the servant. Mary Anne's ears were enchanted with his deep, cultured voice, so unlike her uncle's high-pitched whine. What must he be thinking of us? she wondered.

Lord Edwin deigned to glance at the interloper then and was immediately struck by the fact that he was alone. The smallest parlor in the inn seated four. He stepped forward with a hungry smile and offered his hand. "Tempest in a teapot," he explained. "It seems we've both reserved the same parlor. No reason we must behave like apes and squabble over it. We can act like the civilized gentlemen we are and share it, what? Happy for your company, Mr.—"

The briefest flash of anger flickered over the gentleman's face. Mary Anne, observing, felt this stranger wasn't in the habit of being told what he would do. But while she watched, the anger disappeared, to be replaced by an equally brief flash of cunning. That was the unlikely word that occurred to her. Then the stranger smiled and took Lord Edwin's outstretched hand. She wished she could think the smile had something to do with herself, but she knew it had not. He hadn't even glanced at her.

"Mr. Robertson," the stranger said.

"Lord Edwin Horton of Horton Hall, and this is my niece, Miss Judson."

"I'm very pleased to make your acquaintance, ma'am," Mr. Robertson said with a city bow that had very little in common with the ungainly bobs usually seen in Dymchurch. The thorn bud eyes quickly ran over her toilette, lingering a moment on her face. Mary Anne flushed and smiled nervously. "An eye in him like a tiger," Mrs. Plummer would say.

The servant breathed a sigh of relief and led them to

23

the parlor. As Mr. Robertson held Mary Anne's chair, she noticed that he had a very winning smile, not at all predatory. He had nice white teeth, too, but the special charm of his smile owed more to his eyes than his mouth. The eyes glowed with interest and—was it possible?—admiration.

"Thank you," she said, so softly he didn't hear.

They ordered wine, and Lord Edwin, returned to spirits by his success, became cordial. "Mr. Robertson, what brings you to our fair village? Just passing through, I fancy?"

"Actually I'm visiting a Mr. Vulch."

"Vulch, eh?" Lord Edwin nodded, while he mentally canvassed what such a loftly-looking lad could be doing with old Vulch. The possibilities were numerous. It could be business, politics, or it could be the lad was a relative.

Mary Anne listened eagerly. It cropped into her head that he might have come to court Bess Vulch.

"Are you acquainted with him?" Mr. Robertson asked.

"I know him like a brother. Is he some kin to you?"

"Oh, no. I'm here on business."

"From London, I presume?" Lord Edwin asked, as his eyes roamed over Mr. Robertson's city style. Robertson nodded.

"Whitehall?" Lord Edwin ventured.

"Bond Street," Mr. Robertson said.

This caused Lord Edwin's brow to lift in disparagement. He hadn't planned to share his table with a merchant, but there you were. Never guess it to look at him that he was a hopped-up retailer. If the Cits were frequenting Weston, the *gentlemen* must find a new tailor.

Mr. Robertson noticed the expression and held his own features immobile. "Perhaps you could direct me to Vulch's place," he said. "I understand he doesn't live right in the village, but somewhere west of town."

During the interval till dinner arrived, Lord Edwin confined his conversation to his niece, and Mr. Robertson wrote something in a little black notebook. Figuring out his day's profit, very likely. Once a steaming plate of mutton sat before him, however, Lord Edwin gave up his pretensions to snobbery and became expansive.

"What line of trade are you in, Mr. Robertson?" he asked.

"Drapery."

Mary Anne was hard put to account for the leap of interest in her uncle's eyes. So was Mr. Robertson.

"Drapery, you say." His fingers tapped his cheek in a telltale way that caused his niece to wonder. "Woolens, muslins, *silks* . . . ?"

"Yes," Mr. Robertson said, and lifted his knife and fork, both of which he handled like a gentleman.

"No need to ask further why you're visiting Mr. Vulch, then," Lord Edwin said. "No secret hereabouts, he imports silk." He smiled to himself at that clever use of "import," to denote his acceptance of the practice. Mr. Robertson was no longer despised. He had become a person of great interest, one to be courted as a possible purchaser. Of course, the proposition must be put forward discreetly. Fitch must act as liaison man.

Mary Anne wished to share Mr. Robertson's attention and said, "If you've come to buy the latest shipment, I fear your trip was in vain. It was stolen last night during the storm. The empty lugger was grounded on a sandbar just in front of my uncle's property. When the customs men searched it this morning, the load was gone. They say in the village that Vulch hasn't got it."

"Right in front of your property?" Robertson asked swiftly.

"On our very doorstep," she confirmed. She certainly

25

had his attention now. His eyes were sparkling with curiosity.

"Have you any idea who might have taken it?"

"Vulch is the slyest man in the parish," Lord Edwin announced. "He has it, certainly. What would a thousand ells of silk bring in London?"

Mr. Robertson didn't blink an eye when his companion announced the exact size of the load, but he noticed it. "It would depend on the quality," he said.

"But on the average. Say, for a pretty good-looking lot," Lord Edwin pressed.

"Approximately a thousand pounds," he replied, and watched from under his lashes as Lord Edwin smiled benignly.

"A thousand pounds, eh? Heh, heh. Old Vulch will never miss it. He's rich as Croesus, the old crook."

Mr. Robertson still remained impassive at this revealing speech. Why should he speak of Vulch "never missing it" if Vulch had the stuff? "I'm very interested in recovering the load," he said. "In fact, I'm thinking of offering a reward—say ten percent on top of the purchase price. I can hardly put such a notice in the journals, since smuggling is illegal, but you might spread the word around."

Lord Edwin's fingers patted his cheek. "I'll be sure to tell anyone I'm speaking to." He smiled warmly.

"This is the prime month for selling silk, with the season in progress. I have many orders to be filled. If I don't deliver, I'll lose my customers' future business."

"Yes, yes, I see your problem. Demmed awkward situation for you."

"That's why I rushed down to Dymchurch to look into the matter," Mr. Robertson said, and immediately regretted it. The young girl didn't say much, but she was sharp as a tack.

Mary Anne lifted her eyes and regarded him curiously.

London was a good five or six hours from Dymchurch. Mr. Robertson must have left by noon—and the silk would hardly have had time to reach him. How did he knew it wasn't en route?

He rushed on to eradicate her frown. "I thought I might meet the wagon along the way," he added.

"I'm sure you'll recover it," Lord Edwin said genially. "It can't have gone far, what? You'll be putting up with Vulch, will you—in case I get a line on who has the stuff?"

"I haven't been invited, but I understand he lives in a big way and will be able to accommodate me." Mr. Robertson noticed Lord Edwin's frown. If this fellow had managed to get hold of the cargo, he obviously wouldn't want to sell his stolen goods under Vulch's nose. "Or I could be reached here, at the inn," he added. "I'll be stopping here from time to time to—to pick up my mail," he said in confusion.

"With the big demand for silk at this time," Lord Edwin said, "I wonder if the stuff wouldn't fetch an even higher price in London."

Mr. Robertson rushed in to assure him it would not. The subject of silk was allowed to drop, and the remainder of the meal passed pleasantly. Just before leaving, Mr. Robertson thought he would like to have a look at where the silk vanished and turned his warmest smile on Mary Anne. He noticed then that she was, in fact, attractive.

Her beauty was of the quiet sort that crept up on you, rather than leaping out and assaulting you at one blow. Her eyes were dark and lustrous, but it was her smile that he found particularly winning. It was a soft, shy smile that suited her retiring manner. After the wayward debs of London it was a pleasant change.

To win favor with the uncle, Mr. Robertson reached for the bill when it was presented. "You were kind enough to let me share your table," he said to Lord Edwin. "You must allow me to take care of the bill."

Lord Edwin didn't give him any argument. Once a fellow has paid for your mutton, you could hardly snub him. Lord Edwin smiled his agreement when Mr. Robertson hinted that he would be honored if he might call on Miss Judson tomorrow.

She stared as if she couldn't believe her ears, and looked to her uncle. "That—that would be fine," she said in a voice that squeaked with pleasant embarrassment. Her cheeks flushed bright pink in a way that made Mr. Robertson smile.

They called for their carriages and went out together, surveyed by many curious eyes. A stranger in Dymchurch wasn't interesting per se, but when he stood chatting with Miss Judson and her uncle, he acquired some cachet.

The carriage awaiting the newcomer was a yellow sporting curricle, drawn by a spanking pair of grays. Lord Edwin's eyes roamed lovingly over the team, then turned disconsolately to his own sadly matched pair of jades. "That's a dandy set of prads," he said. "I daresay a team like that would set a fellow back a pretty penny at Tattersall's." Imagine a Cit having such a bang-up team.

"They don't come cheap, but you get what you pay for," Robertson answered nonchalantly.

Lord Edwin patted the nags a minute, then said, "I'll have my driver draw to a halt when we come to Vulch's side road. You turn right there and go a quarter of a mile down a crinkum-crankum road to the house. A great pretentious thing with half a dozen bow windows. You can't miss it. Good night, Mr. Robertson. Nice to have met you."

Mr. Robertson bowed and returned the civility. Before leaving, he said to Mary Anne, "And how do I reach your house, Miss Judson? How shall I recognize it tomorrow?"

"Horton Hall is a mile farther along this road. It's an old run-down Tudor home," she said. Her frankness amused him. No putting on airs. Like a real lady, she stated the truth without shame.

A pity he'd be so busy. He felt he could learn to cherish this Miss Judson with the sweet smile. After he settled his business, he might linger a day or two. But business before pleasure—and what the devil could have happened to the cargo?

In the carriage Mary Anne said, "He seemed very nice."

"A bang-up team."

Lord Edwin stopped his dilatory team at Vulch's road, and he and Mary Anne craned their necks to see that the yellow curricle made the proper turn before they continued on their way. Mr. Roberton lifted his curled beaver and bowed.

At Horton Hall Mrs. Plummer had set the table with care and kept the chicken warm for an hour, hoping it wasn't destroyed. She had begun to suspect it wouldn't be eaten that night. You'd think people could tell you if they didn't plan to take dinner at home, she mused, but in her heart she was so happy Mary Anne had had an outing that she didn't plan to scold.

"I hope you didn't hold dinner for us," were the first words Miss Judson said when she came in. She could smell the aroma of roasted chicken in the air and suspected there would be a cake as well. "We ate at the inn, Mrs. Plummer. It was crowded to the rafters. We went to Folkestone and stopped at all the villages on the way home. We had lunch at Bates, and had a wonderful day. We met a man at the inn."

A person couldn't deliver a lecture after that outpouring, so Mrs. Plummer said she was happy to hear it. "I'll cover the chicken I roasted up, to keep the mouse from it, and serve it cold tomorrow.''

"Did anything happen here?" Mary Anne asked.

"Belle ate through her rope again and got into the home garden to gobble up anything that survived her last rooting. We need a steel chain for the beast. Other than that, it's been so quiet you could hear the termites gnawing."

"I see the lugger is gone from the bay," Lord Edwin said. It was the second thing he noticed as he came in. The first was that the hay wain didn't appear to have been tampered with.

"They had the tug pull it free this afternoon," Mrs. Plummer told him. "Codey was here again asking questions and looking all around."

Lord Edwin jumped a foot. "Eh, looking all around? What do you mean? You said all was quiet."

"He didn't come to the house. He hired a couple of his cousins as assistants and had them search the stables and barn and icehouse. He thought the smugglers might have hidden the silk here, as the boat was grounded so close."

Lord Edwin jumped like a gaffed fish. "They didn't find anything!"

"What is there to find?" Plummer asked in a purely rhetorical spirit. She knew better than any how empty were the stalls and stables of Horton Hall.

"I must have a word with Fitch," Lord Edwin said, and went scampering upstairs.

Mary Anne regaled Mrs. Plummer with more details of her day till he returned. The name Mr. Robertson cropped up at every second phrase. "I'll have to use two pages of my diary tonight," she finished happily.

"One on this Mr. Robertson, eh, missie?" Mrs. Plummer teased. "He sounds quite a swell. It figures, a draper would wear a fine jacket."

"I couldn't do him justice in one page. I wager Bess Vulch will throw her bonnet at him."

"Ho, that trollop would chase after anything in trousers. What did your uncle buy you for your birthday?"

"I don't know," Mary Anne said, frowning. "We were in half a dozen shops, but I didn't see him come out with anything. I fancy he had Jem pick it up after we left. He's probably wrapping it right now. I think it might be material for a new gown," Mary Anne said. A hopeful smile lit her eyes on this daring wish. "Do you think we could get it made up by Saturday, Mrs. Plummer? I'd like to wear it to the spring assembly."

"We'll stitch to beat the devil. Between the two of us, we'll manage."

Lord Edwin wore a kindly smile when he returned with a parcel all nicely done up in white paper and pink ribbons. It was his brief talk with Fitch that accounted for his good humor. That maw-worm of a Codey hadn't even looked at the hay wain. Stood beside it, actually leaning on it while he discussed with Fitch where the silk could be. Fitch had led him a merry chase.

"Happy birthday, my dear," he said, and handed Mary Anne the parcel.

They went into the Blue Saloon for the unwrapping. Mary Anne's fingers trembled with excitement as she carefully untied the pink ribbons and lifted the lid of the box. She stared in wonder at the exquisite piece of fabric it contained. It shimmered a pale gold, but that wasn't even the half of it. As she unfolded it, she saw the intricate needlework and gasped in pleasure. Flowers and birds and trees all swirled together to form a beautiful pattern.

"Oh, Uncle! Where did you get it? It's *beautiful*! Look, Mrs. Plummer," she said, and wrapped herself in the lovely shawl. "And the fringe—it must be three inches long. I'll be the most fashionable lady at the assembly."

Lord Edwin felt a jolt of surprise at this speech. The demmed assembly was only a few days away. Would anyone recognize the shawl? No, how could they? Only Fitch and he had seen it. Did Vulch know a shawl would be in the load? He had forgotten the assembly was so close. He could hardly ask Mary Anne not to wear it. He smiled nervously and said, "Happy you like it. What do you think, eh, Plummer?"

Mrs. Plummer put on her spectacles to view the embroidery. She fancied herself as good a woman as any with her needle, but she'd never tackled anything this complicated. "Very nice," she allowed mildly. The admission was gall to her pride. "Odd, the way it's done. I wouldn't have used a cross-stich on a tree myself, but it looks mighty fine. And see the way the leaves are done in knots. Blue leaves mixed with gold and green—what kind of tree is that supposed to be?"

Mary Anne examined the design more carefully. "It gives the effect of shadows and sunlight," she pointed out. "It's a real work of art. Wherever did you buy it, Uncle?"

"I picked it up at Folkestone," he lied amiably.

"But why did you stop at the drapery shops in Hythe and Sandgate after?" his niece asked.

He scowled at this close questioning. "I was looking for a pair of gloves to go with it but couldn't find them," he said.

"Your kid gloves will be fine," Mrs. Plummer assured Mary Anne. "No one will notice the spotty fingers if you keep your hands closed."

"I'm going to go up and try my shawl with my blue gown," Mary Anne said, and ran upstairs. On the way out she stopped and hugged her uncle. "This is the best birthday I ever had! Thank you, darling Uncle Edwin."

Lord Edwin jiggled in embarrassment and backed away.

She didn't actually put her blue gown on, but by hanging

the shawl over the gown, she could see it was beautiful, especially from the back, where the design showed best. While she was doing this, there was a tap at her door. She went, expecting Mrs. Plummer, and met Fitch, who handed her another small parcel.

"Happy birthday, Miss Judson. I wish it could be more."

She thanked him and opened the little box while he waited, shifting from left foot to right in anxiety that his gift would find favor. After long discourse with Mrs. Plummer, he had bought a new patent pen to go with the diary. She had eked a few pennies from the kitchen money for the purpose.

Mary Anne smiled in pleasure. She felt hot tears fill her eyes at this token of friendship. She wanted to hug Fitch but knew this would be exceeding the bounds of acceptable behavior. Fitch was only twenty-five, and as he was very handsome, they had to keep their distance. So she just smiled and thanked him profusely.

When he left, she laid her three gifts out on her bed and smiled at them for a long time. Visions whirled through her head. Memories of the day, and of Mr. Robertson. Plans for the future, especially the assembly. She hoped Mr. Robertson would still be here. The best part of the whole birthday was that Joseph Horton hadn't come to call.

Just as she was thanking fate for this, Mrs. Plummer came tapping at the door. "It's Mr. Horton to see you, Miss Judson," she said.

Well, you couldn't expect a day to be perfect.

Chapter Four

Mary Anne's hand hovered over the shawl. No, she wouldn't bother wearing it to impress Joseph. She'd save it for the assembly. She went downstairs still wearing her afternoon gown and saw Joseph standing in the doorway of the saloon, waiting for her. He had a fine physique, tall and well formed, but when he smiled, there was no light in his pale gray eyes. His sluggish complexion compared unfavorably to the weathered hues of Mr. Robertson. There was no hint of chestnut in his black hair and no charm in his whole body.

"Good evening, Mary Anne. I came to wish you a happy birthday." He smiled. She saw the telltale box in his fingers. It looked the size of a ring box, and something in her tightened to revulsion.

"You shouldn't have bothered, Joseph," she answered coolly.

"It's no bother. I've already been here once today. Fitch told me you were out. I didn't know you were planning an outing or I would have arranged to go with you."

"It wasn't planned. We decided on the spur of the moment."

"That's Lord Edwin all over—dashing off half-cocked."

34

She gave him a scathing look and took up her seat on a chair so he couldn't sit too close to her.

"You ought to have a chaperon," Joseph said.

"Mrs. Plummer will be here shortly. I believe she's gone to make tea."

With the proprieties arranged, Joseph sat on the end of the sofa closest to her chair. "I've bought you a little something," he said, and handed her the box.

"Thank you." She accepted it with a heavy heart. "What is it?" she asked suspiciously.

"You'll have to open it and see."

She pulled at the strings and slowly undid the paper. It was a ring, as she feared, but it was a very plain little ring, with a row of tiny seed pearls across the top. Actually a pretty ring, but before trying it on, she wanted to make sure it came burdened with no symbolism.

Mr. Horton, who had a very good opinion of himself, misunderstood her drooping lips. "Not what you expected, I daresay," he said in a consoling way. "I would like to have given you an engagement ring, Mary Anne, but—"

"No! No, it's—it's lovely, Joseph," she said quickly, and put it on.

"As I was saying, I wanted to give you an engagement ring, but Mama feels till I have paid off the mortgage, it would be premature. As you have no dowry, you know . . ."

"We're not engaged. Why on earth would you think of giving me an engagement ring?"

"I think you know my feelings, at any rate."

Mrs. Plummer arrived with the tea tray, and Joseph's tepid lovemaking came to a halt. "Where is Lord Edwin tonight?" he asked.

As he spoke, there was a knock at the door, causing everyone to jump. Night callers at Horton Hall were rare.

The most usual one was already with them. "Who can that be?" Mr. Horton asked. He sounded rather peevish. "And where is Fitch? I don't know how you put up with this place, Mrs. Plummer. A butler who is never around when you need him. Only your poor self to try to keep this shambles of a house from falling apart."

Commiseration from any other source than Joseph Horton was as welcome as desert rain. Coming from him, it was considered an impertinence. Mrs. Plummer went to answer the door without a word, and Mr. Horton cast a condemning glance around the room.

"I saw a sheet of lead on the ground this afternoon, too. It's fallen off the roof. I mean to have a word with Lord Edwin about that. He might at least keep a roof on my inheritance."

Mary Anne had stopped listening to him, or he might have received a rebuke for this comment. She had discerned the unmistakable accents of Mr. Robertson at the doorway and could hardly believe her ears. She wildly conjectured what could have happened. The Vulches weren't home, and Mr. Robertson had come here! Oh, dear, would he expect to stay the night? Her mind flew to unaired bedrooms, half of them with mildewed carpets, and none of them made up.

As she sat transfixed, she heard another voice, Mr. Vulch's. "Could I have a word with Lord Edwin, Mrs. Plummer?" he said in his pained way. Why the richest and most powerful man in the parish should have such a whining manner was hard to understand. Vulch didn't look important. He looked like a lackey, with his dilapidated face, pouchy eyes, and shifty manner.

Mrs. Plummer showed the guests in. Mary Anne turned instinctively to Mr. Robertson. He looked exactly as she remembered him. He even wore the same expression—one of warm interest. Like a true gentleman, he hardly examined the sad disrepair of the chamber.

"Joseph, this is Mr. Robertson," she said, flustered. "Mr. Horton is my cousin," she explained to the guest.

"Robertson, you say?" Joseph asked. He was examining the caller with a questioning look. "Have we met before, sir?"

"Mr. Robertson is from London," Mary Anne said.

Joseph went up to London as often as he could find an excuse. The face before him certainly looked familiar, yet not familiar enough that he could put a name to it.

Mr. Robertson smiled blandly and said, "Perhaps you've been in my shop. I run the Robertson Drapery Shop on Bond Street."

"Drapery shop!" Joseph exclaimed, while his eyes made a quick but accurate assessment of the man's toilette. If this fellow was a draper, he was a yahoo.

"It's a family business. My father, and his father before him, sold draperies. First from a simple monger's wagon, but in '79, my father hired a store," Mr. Robertson said, and seemed prepared to continue in this vein.

Mary Anne was pleased that he made no effort to conceal his origins and annoyed that Joseph had stiffened to a perfect board of disapproval.

"Very interesting, I'm sure," Joseph said satirically.

"We have our woolens on sale at the moment—out of season, you know. I could put you in the way of some excellent worsted if—"

Joseph lifted his brows and pinched his nose. "I'm not in the habit of haggling for wool during a social visit, Mr. Robinson."

"That's 'Robertson,' " Mary Anne said angrily. Really, she was as annoyed with Robertson as with Joseph. His manners had been much better at the inn. She sensed he was just doing it to roast the toplofty Joseph.

37

Naturally she was curious to hear what had brought this party calling, and soon learned that it was Lord Edwin they wished to see. He was sent for, and till he arrived, the mismatched group sat chatting of the weather and other bland nothings. She observed Joseph's surreptitious examination of Mr. Robertson. Mr. Robertson also noticed it and began sprinkling his conversation with a few low phrases.

"I've a dandy bargain you might want to get in on, Miss Judson," he said. "Kerseymere—a touch out of fashion, which is why I could let you have a few ells for an old song."

"I don't get up to London very often," she parried.

"I could ship it to you, F.O.B. Dymchurch."

"Miss Judson has already told you she isn't interested!" Joseph said.

"Nay, she only told me she doesn't get up to London very often. A pity," he said, with a laughing look at her.

When Lord Edwin joined the party, Joseph stood up and made his apologies. "I don't like to leave Mama alone too long," he gave as an excuse. It had, in fact, just occurred to him that with Mr. Vulch there, Miss Vulch might be happy for his company. His conscience told him he owed an offer to Mary Anne—a penniless cousin, after all, and what would come of her when Lord Edwin stuck his spoon in the wall? Another corner of his mind whispered that Miss Vulch was the most eligible parti in the county, and not at all averse to him, if her smiles were any indication of her feelings.

As Joseph headed for the door, Mr. Robertson jumped up and went after him. "Mr. Horton! Did I give you the address of my shop in London?" he called.

Mary Anne bit back her smile and waited till he returned. "That was doing it pretty brown, Mr. Robertson," she said. "Literally running after business."

"I didn't want to disappoint him. He's not so immune to a bargain as he would like the world to believe. He's agreed to accept some samples of my stuff."

"I trust they will be better than the genteel sample of hawking you purveyed this evening."

"I'll send ye a batch, too, if ye'd care to sample my wares," he said, with a laughing eye that made her flush.

Vulch had only waited till the front door closed before turning his drooping eyes to Lord Edwin. "Now that he's gone, we can get on with it. We want to know what happened to that cargo of silk, Lord Eddie." There was a hint of anger, or accusation, in his manner.

Lord Edwin blinked in astonishment. "We would all like to know that. Just between us and the bedpost, you have it safely put away, eh, Vulch? Had your fellows spirit it off in the dark of night."

"No, sir, I did not. I don't have it. It wasn't unloaded when those fool Frenchies abandoned ship. It went astray at your very doorstep between one o'clock this morning and five-thirty when Codey got aboard and searched the lugger."

"Well, it didn't go astray here!" Lord Edwin assured him. He felt truly outraged that his character should be assailed by this commoner. That the implied charge was true didn't detract a jot from his anger. His dark eyes flashed with a noble fire, and his nostrils flared.

Mary Anne shared his outrage. "Mr. Vulch, are you suggesting my uncle had something to do with the disappearance of the silk?" she demanded.

Mr. Robertson examined their host and decided he was out in his reading of Lord Edwin. The man didn't have the silk. Perhaps it was common knowledge that the stuff came a thousand ells to a cargo. "I'm sure that wasn't Mr. Vulch's meaning," he said calmly. "We only came to in-

39

quire if you had seen or heard anything that might indicate who took it.''

Lord Edwin turned a curious eye on Robertson. "Nothing," he said firmly. "I told you I would mention your reward of ten percent to anyone I met."

"We had hoped you might have seen or heard the disturbance when the goods were stolen," Mr. Robertson continued. "Horses or the sound of a wagon. If we even had an idea which direction the thieves took . . ."

Lord Edwin shook his head. "If Vulch don't have it, I fancy it was pirated by another ship. Where you ought to turn your investigation is to the docks. Take my word for it, the silk will have the scent of fish when you find it."

Robertson listened with interest, but Vulch, more intimate with Lord Edwin's rudimentary conscience, was still unconvinced. "You won't mind if we have a look around your place tomorrow?"

"Codey's been over the place with a fine-tooth comb and found nothing." Lord Edwin stretched his arms along the back of the sofa, the perfect picture of ease, and said, "I wish I could offer you a glass of brandy, but unfortunately this niece of mine won't let me have smuggled merchandise in the house." He gave Vulch an accusing glance with this pious speech.

Mary Anne blinked to learn she was the cause of his deprivation. With a mind to the cake in the kitchen, she said, "Perhaps the gentlemen would like some tea instead, Uncle."

"An excellent idea. Ring for Plummer."

"I'll speak to her," Mary Anne said, and hopped up. She wanted to oversee this important tea herself, and make sure all the best china was used.

During the interim Vulch and Lord Edwin fell into a political argument, and when the tea came, Mary Anne found she had Mr. Robertson to herself. After a little small talk, he said, "I expect all the smuggling lore is as well known as an old ballad here on the coast. Who the smugglers are, what amounts are brought in, what price is got for the goods, and so on?"

"One hears talk," she agreed. "They usually bring in twenty barrels to a load."

"And the silk?"

"We don't hear so much about that," she replied. "Uncle isn't interested in the silk, you see."

"Yet he knew a thousand ells were on the lugger," he pointed out.

She gave him a curious, thoughtful look. "Yes, he did. It was being discussed at the inn. That must be where he heard it."

"I also audited the gossip at the inn. No one mentioned the quantity. Another manner of learning it suggests itself," he said leadingly. "It was abandoned on your uncle's very doorstep. Before you fly into the boughs, let me make clear I'm not suggesting your uncle took it. Only that he might have seen or overheard something—from his servants perhaps, or a friend that he wouldn't willingly betray." He stopped, looking to see if the lady took umbrage at this lesser charge. Her expression was difficult to interpret. She wasn't outraged, at least, but more . . . thoughtful.

Oh, Lord, she thought. All day Uncle's been behaving most strangely. All those trips to drapers in Folkestone and the other towns. The meetings in private offices with store managers. *Uncle had stolen the cargo!* Somewhere on the few acres that comprised this estate he had concealed stolen merchandise. It was true, he mentioned a thousand ells, and how did he knew that if he didn't have it? It explained his good humor all day long, and his delight to learn Mr. Robertson was a drapery merchant.

"He said he had not," she answered with some composure. "There was a dreadful storm, you know. The rain and thunder would have made hearing impossible, even if he had been awake. And, naturally, he wouldn't go out on such a night, so how could he have seen anything? I certainly heard nothing," she added. As she spoke, her mind ran off in other directions. *What has he done with it? Where has he hidden the cargo? A thousand ells of silk must be very cumbersome. Oh, dear, and if he's caught, we're ruined.* She felt as if she were sitting on a keg of gunpowder that might go off at any moment and blow them all to oblivion.

Of one thing she was very sure. Lord Edwin must not get caught in his thievery. She would endeavor to persuade him to return the stolen goods—a bootless chore, she feared—but she would do anything in her power to protect him. Devotion to her uncle was not the only motive for her tacit vow. Of equal importance was that Mr. Robertson not learn her uncle was a thief.

"Is it remotely possible your servants might be involved?" he asked.

"I shouldn't think Fitch would do it alone, and Mrs. Plummer would hardly turn smuggler," she answered, smiling to think of portly Plummer striking out to sea. Fitch, of course, would have had to do the hard labor.

"And the others?" he pressed.

"Others?" Mary Anne blinked in confusion. "Oh, there are no others. We hobble along on two servants. Uncle hasn't much money," she confided. "A younger son, you know, and Whitehall has been very mean about withholding his pension."

"He's in the basket, then?"

"Always," she answered bluntly. "But that is not to say he is a thief!"

"Well, someone in the neighborhood is," Robertson

said. "How about that chap who was leaving when we arrived?"

"Joseph Horton, my uncle's heir. No," she said, smiling at the incongruity of it. "Joseph hasn't the gumption to say boo to a goose."

Little dimples appeared at the corner of her lips when she smiled in that particular way. Mr. Robertson found himself smiling, too. "I gather it was your fair self Joseph was calling on, then, and protecting so feverishly from a merchant."

She looked at the little pearl ring and said, "Yes," in a dispirited way. "He often calls on me. I fear he's quite immune to a snub."

"Merchants' manners!"

Raised voices on the other side of the room interrupted their conversation. "By God, you don't fool me, Horton!" Mr. Vulch shouted. "You've got my stuff, and I'll have a search warrant here tomorrow to search you from attics to cellars. And a guard posted to see it isn't moved, too. You're going to get caught red-handed. You may count yourself fortunate if you don't hang for this."

Lord Edwin jumped to his feet. His narrow face was red with anger. "Call in the law to recover your *smuggled* goods that have no right being in the country? I think not, my good fellow. By God, the world is in a fine state when a smuggler calls a nobleman a thief in his own house. I'll thank you and your merchant friend to vacate my premises. Immediately!"

"There's more at stake here than a cargo of smuggled silk!" Vulch shouted.

Mr. Robertson's face pinched in alarm, and he jumped up from the sofa. "That'll do, Vulch!" he exclaimed. His tone was not that of a merchant come begging for help. It had the accent of authority. Vulch looked at him, and a look of guilty anger was on his face.

Mary Anne looked from one to the other, wondering. What did Mr. Robertson mean? And why did Vulch fall silent at his command?

"We'll go now," Mr. Robertson said stiffly.

Lord Edwin sniffed and turned his head aside, as though he could no longer tolerate the sight of his guests. Mr. Robertson had the sangfroid to thank his hostess before leaving.

With a twinkling smile he added, "I rather think this precludes my calling on you tomorrow, as I hoped to do. I shall be loitering in front of the inn at Dymchurch tomorrow afternoon at two, however, if you find you need to make a few purchases. Ribbons, silk . . ." he added daringly.

A gurgle of laughter caught in her throat. The gentlemen left, and Mary Anne turned a sapient eye on her uncle. "Where did you hide it?" she asked.

"Hide what?"

"The silk. Where is it, Uncle? Your best bet is to dump it in the sea and let the tide wash it out."

"Now my own niece is accusing me! I resent that very much, Mary Anne," Lord Edwin said with a glare that combined pain and indignation in equal quantity. Of shame there was not a trace.

"I was sure you had taken it," she said uncertainly. "How did you know the shipment was a thousand ells?"

"It always is. I've heard Vulch bragging about his hauls till I'm tired to death of it."

"And why were you in all the drapers' offices this morning having those private meetings? That wasn't necessary, only to buy a shawl."

Lord Edwin didn't blink before answering. He had foreseen the question, once the subject of his culpability arose. "Very well, then," he said, eyes staring reproachfully, "if you will insist on humiliating me, I bought the shawl on

44

tick. I hadn't the cash to pay for it. I had hoped to buy a length of silk to go with it, which is why I visited the other shops after buying your shawl at Folkestone. Things have come to a fine pass when my own niece questions my integrity," he added, plunging the dagger to the hilt.

Mary Anne felt the full burden of shame for having suspected him, which was precisely what he intended. "I'm sorry, Uncle," she said meekly. How awful of her to have accused him. She felt a very ingrate, almost a sinner. "I mean I'm glad you didn't do it, but I'm sorry I accused you."

Lord Edwin gave a forgiving nod.

"I wonder what Vulch meant when he said this incident involves more than a cargo of silk?" Mary Anne mentioned.

"I expect the loss jeopardizes his whole operation. The Frenchies aren't going to send their stuff over to a ninny who loses it, now, are they?"

Lord Edwin was eager to quit the conversation, and arose. "I must see Fitch," he said, and added to divert fresh suspicion, "about securing the doors. We don't want smugglers landing in on us while we sleep."

He turned and sped from the room. Mary Anne was relieved that her uncle wasn't the thief, but she was sorry for having given voice to her doubts. She also regretted the contretemps that had arisen between him and Mr. Robertson. Uncle Edwin had a short temper but a forgiving nature withal. He'd have forgotten both arguments by tomorrow. Perhaps he'd even take her into Dymchurch after lunch. About two, Mr. Robertson had said. She went upstairs and began writing in her new diary.

Chapter Five

In the fine spring weather Mary Anne often went for a ride in the morning. She didn't have a mount, but Uncle Edwin had taught her to ride on his own bay mare, Bingo, so named for the color of her hide, a tawny amber, the shade of his favorite drink. With age, the brandy color had faded till Badger would have been a more appropriate name, but Bingo's senile gait suited Mary Anne's mood that morning. All she wanted was an amble through the pasture and meadow to look at the flowers and feel the warm sun on her shoulders while she daydreamed of Mr. Robertson.

"I wouldn't venture too far afield on that old jade," Plummer cautioned. "Bingo couldn't outrun a sloth if you was to be chased. With that silk still unaccounted for, God knows who's lurking about seeking to devour us."

"We've been searched by Codey. It's not here, Mrs. Plummer. I don't think we have to worry."

"Fitch and your uncle are acting mighty odd. I don't know that they're not in on it."

"I expect they're looking for it. Mr. Robertson has offered a reward of ten percent, you know."

"That'd be it." Plummer nodded. She didn't really think her employer was sharp enough to have engineered the piracy.

As Fitch wasn't to be seen, Mary Anne saddled up Bingo herself and led her past the home garden carefully, to avoid trampling what remained of it after Belle's depredations. Everything looked so fresh and beautiful that day, with the sun shining on new greenery everywhere and the sky a perfect azure. It almost seemed an omen, that cloudless sky. Except that on her personal horizon she would have scattered a few wisps of gray. Joseph Horton, for instance, and her uncle's little spat with Mr. Robertson. Bess Vulch, too, presented a possible disruption of her cloudless future.

She jogged along through the meadow and had to dismount to open the pasture gate. Bingo's jumping days were over, poor old mare. Bessie, the sole remaining cow from their herd, lifted her head from grazing to greet Bingo as she passed by. They went out the gate on the far side of the pasture and on to Mr. Christian's land. He was an old friend and took no exception to his neighbors' exercising the mare there. Mary Anne's favorite course was to follow the stream, often stopping to gather the wildflowers that grew profusely in that well-watered stretch of land.

The bluebells were at their peak. She'd stop on her way back and take home a bouquet for the table. The daisies would look well as a contrast. The hyacinths were her favorite, but she knew of old that these were only to be culled by Mrs. Christian, who had planted them for their fragrant perfume. She could smell it wafting on the breeze, as strong as cologne. On a whim, she dismounted to smell the hyacinths.

Trouble was the furthest thing from Mary Anne's mind on this perfect day. She knelt down and buried her nose in the patch of flowers, inhaling deeply. Just as she was about to rise, she noticed the fresh imprint of hooves in the soft earth. With the missing silk at the back of her mind, she wondered if it might be hidden nearby. The

47

imprints looked as if they had been made by two or three horses.

Her heart beat heavily as she looked all around, listening for the sound of an intruder. Only the gurgling of the stream and the cheeping of new birds in the nest interrupted the silence. Was the silk here? Where could they have hidden it? There was no building or cave nearby, but it could be concealed amongst the trees, which offered some protection. She tied Bingo to the closest tree and edged slowly forward, following the horse tracks. They didn't cross the stream but veered eastward toward the old shepherd's hut a quarter of a mile farther along. A perfect hiding place!

Her heartbeats grew heavy and her legs shook. What if she found the silk! A reward of a hundred pounds, or possibly guineas! She could have the roof fixed and stop Joseph's griping. As she came to the edge of the trees, the little thatch-roofed hut came into view. There were no mounts tethered outside it, but the tracks led directly to the door. They'd been and left. She'd steal up and just make sure the silk was there.

After watching for a few minutes to see that no one was coming, she crept silently from the shelter of the trees and approached the hut. She was still several yards from it when a horse neighed, sending her into alarm. The sound came from the far side of the hut. She froze in her tracks, and as she stood, a dark head peeped out of the doorway.

''Nom d'un nom! C'est une fille! Arrêtez-elle!'' the man shouted.

Mary Anne's French was rudimentary, but instinct told her that flight was her best course. She took to her heels and flew like the wind, with a large man following closely behind her. As she darted through the trees, not stopping to look behind her, the sound of his footfalls drew closer and closer. She ran faster, but her skirts made outrunning him impossible. He caught up with her just as she reached Bingo. His rough hands came out and grabbed her around the waist, turning her toward him.

She saw then, through her terror, that he was a youngish man. His roughly tousled hair and saturnine expression robbed him of charm, but his features were regular.

His panting breaths fanned her cheek. *"Quelle jolie fille!"* He smiled and tightened his grip around her waist.

"Let go of me!" she exclaimed in a voice quavering with panic.

"Pourquoi es-tu ici?" he asked.

"I don't know what you're saying. I don't understand," she gasped, squirming to free herself, which only made the man tighten his grip till she was pressed close against his chest. It was warm and damp from the chase. The animal smell of masculine sweat was in her nostrils, adding to her fright.

"La soie!" he exclaimed. "Silk."

"Silk?" she repeated, trying to give the illusion she knew nothing of it and cared less. *"Je ne sais pas."* That phrase at least survived from her schoolgirl's lessons.

A smile parted the man's lips, and his black eyes gleamed with mischief. *"C'est trop mal, ma petite. Ah, comme tu es belle,"* he added in a voice that was becoming dangerously amorous. As he spoke, his lips inclined to hers, and one hand went out to hold her head in place.

She wrenched her head aside and hollered at the top of her lungs, "Help!" This was accompanied by a stout kick in his shins that set him to cursing. But he didn't lose track of his object.

Just as his hot lips touched hers, Mary Anne heard the sound of running footsteps. They came from the direction of the hut. She felt in her bones it was his companion, and her heart shriveled in panic. Two of them! Good God, she wished she were dead. Any inhabitant of the coast knew

49

what the Frenchies did with their English victims, especially female victims.

A cultured voice cut through the air like a whip. *"Ça sera assez, monsieur!"*

The words meant nothing to Mary Anne, but she recognized that authoritative voice and her heart swelled in relief. The Frenchman released her at once and lifted his hands in capitulation. A stream of apologetic sounds issued from his lips, accompanied by penitent smiles.

"Allez-vous en," Mr. Robertson said. Mary Anne turned to see that he was really there and not a figment of her overwrought imagination. The pistol in his hand accounted for the Frenchman's hasty departure.

The Frenchman scooted away, back to the hut. Mary Anne was trembling so violently that she could hardly stand up. Now that the ordeal was over, tears of relief sprang to her eyes, and she shivered violently.

"Are you all right?" Robertson demanded in a harsh voice. A hiccuping sob was his answer.

He pulled her into his arms to comfort her with soothing words of reassurance. How vastly different was the experience of being in Mr. Robertson's embrace from that of the Frenchie. The gentle pat of his hand on her shoulder, the firm but unmenacing feel of his arms around her waist, the tender concern in his voice—all were designed to calm her down, and all failed most miserably. The excitement, though pleasurable, was almost unbearable. Something in the episode reminded her of the day Uncle had rescued her from the orphanage.

"There, there, it's fine, Mary Anne," he said, and smiled encouragingly down at her. How beautiful his eyes looked, shadowed with long lashes. "You're going to be all right," he said, and loosened his arms.

"So foolish of me," she said.

"What were you doing here alone?"

"I was just—the hyacinths," she said, and pulled herself from his arms with a flush of embarrassment. "Smelling them—so pretty. I saw the horse tracks leading to the hut. I couldn't see the horses and thought the silk might be hidden there."

"It's not."

Mary Anne looked toward the hut. "We'd best escape while we can," she said with a nervous look all around.

Mr. Robertson gave an indifferent smile. She noticed he was still holding the pistol. He stuck it into his waistband. "I don't think they'll bother us."

"What were you doing here, Mr. Robertson?"

"Scouting around for my silk. This positively confirms that the Frenchies haven't found it. I left my mount at Christian's and was eavesdropping at the hut. I'll pick the horse up later."

He untied Bingo and they began to walk back toward Horton Hall. "Uncle doesn't have it, either," she told him. "I asked him last night. It can't be far away."

"It could conceivably be in London by now," he countered, "but somehow I don't think so."

"What did Vulch mean last night when he said there was more than just a lost cargo involved here?"

He hesitated a moment before answering. Mary Anne's looking for the silk convinced him of her innocence. Any local ally would be helpful, and he could enlist her aid without revealing official secrets.

"His reputation, perhaps," he said nonchalantly. "I for one won't patronize an uncertain source."

"That's what Uncle thought," she said, and accepted it as truth. "The Frenchies don't have the silk, you said?"

"No, they spent the night in Vulch's stable. I followed them this morning. They're out looking for it, like me. But I hope, in future, you will confine your search to Horton Hall. Did you happen to have a look around the house?"

"Mr. Robertson!" she snapped, "I've told you Uncle doesn't have it."

"Vulch thinks otherwise. It might be worth your while at least to look. Perhaps someone else hid it there. Ten percent of a thousand pounds is worth a look," he tempted. "It would buy you a new mount," he added, as it was borne in on him that the one he was leading was decrepit.

"Or a new roof." She sighed. "A sheet of lead came down in the storm." She thought of the reward and said reluctantly, "Well, I'll have a look at home, but I know I shan't find it."

"How can I be in touch with you?"

"Will you be at the assembly Saturday evening?" she asked slyly.

"Good God, I can't wait that long! I meant today. The inn, at two?" he reminded her.

"If I can get the carriage. I can't walk."

"And I can hardly call for you after being hinted away. You could send me a note at Vulch's place if you find anything."

This speech indicated pretty clearly that it was the silk he was interested in and not herself. When she replied, there was a chill in her voice. "If you don't hear from me, you may assume I didn't find anything. I shouldn't think you'll be hearing from me."

"Pity," he murmured, and smiled softly.

They stopped then, at the edge of Mr. Christian's land. Before them was the pasture gate and open ground. She felt he would leave her there, safe on her uncle's property. She disliked to part on this sour note, with no assurance of ever seeing him again.

"Well, thank you for rescuing me," she said with the

small smile that activated the dimples at the corners of her lips. He noticed the dimples vanished when her mouth was open, but those prim, closed-mouth smiles were delightful.

"Perhaps I should see you safely to your door."

"I'll be all right now. This is our pasture—you can see Horton Hall," she said, pointing to it.

The patch where the lead sheeting had fallen was visible from this direction. The sheets that still adhered to the roof were rusted around the edges and coming loose. Mr. Robertson felt a stab of pity for a young lady who would spend her reward on a piece of lead. He had already discovered Mary Anne's circumstances from Vulch, but asking her gave him an excuse to linger.

There was some charm in this idyllic country setting, far from the intrigues and affairs of London drawing rooms that were his more usual haunt. "Have you lived with your uncle long?" he asked.

"For as long as I can remember. My mama was his wife's sister. Uncle Edwin made an unwise match, which is why he is so dreadfully poor. Younger sons should marry wisely, I suppose."

"And your own father?"

"Papa was a younger son, too. He tried to raise horses in Ireland. He got thrown from a wild buck he was trying to tame and broke his neck. That's when Mama came back to England. Uncle Edwin says she should have bought a small property with Papa's money, but she was restless. She lived in Bath for a spell, then Brighton. But I don't remember any of that. She died when I was four, and that's when Uncle Edwin took me in. Really, it was Aunt Hattie who took me, but then she died, too, a few years later, so it's just Uncle and I alone now."

Mr. Robertson listened closely to this tale of woe. One aspect of it smote him more closely than the rest.

"Younger sons should marry wisely." Truer words were never spoken, but it was also true that an elder son was expected to garner himself a noble heiress. A man in his situation was not expected to bring home a penniless bride.

Mary Anne noticed the expression he wore and brought forth for his consideration her sole advantage. "I'm connected to some highly placed people through Uncle Edwin," she said baldly. "His older brother, Lord Exholme, is an earl with a fine estate in Sussex. We visited Longcourt one Christmas. They have a ballroom and everything, but I was too young at the time to attend the ball. Is all your family in trade, Mr. Robertson?" she asked, to highlight the difference in their connections.

"Only I have sunk so low," he told her. One Christmas visit told him pretty clearly that Exholme didn't acknowledge the girl.

"I expect there's a good living in it."

"At least my roof is in good repair," he riposted.

"Bess Vulch is very pretty, don't you think?" was her next remark.

Mr. Robertson had no difficulty following her reasoning. "A pleasant girl," he answered vaguely.

"She has a dot of ten thousand and is very popular hereabouts."

"I'll wager she is," he replied, and laughed aloud at her transparent musings. "But then, of course, she has no highly placed connections."

"Her papa is an M.P."

"Yes, quite. I had forgotten that advantage. Take care she don't nab Joseph while you're out flirting with Frenchies. He was there last night when we returned, you know."

Far from taking offense, Mary Anne's face lit up like the sun. "Was he really? How splendid!"

54

"Are you and Joseph not—how shall I word it discreetly—are you two not courting?"

"Well," she said, frowning over their situation, "he's trying to, I think, but I don't care for him, and Uncle hates his interfering ways, so it doesn't seem to be coming to a head." She glanced at the little pearl ring and spun it around on her finger.

Twenty-four years old. "Perhaps I'll have him in the end," she said disconsolately.

Mr. Robertson observed the downturn of her pretty lips and felt a pronounced aversion to Joseph Horton, whose self-righteous prosing the night before had repelled him.

"I take it that catastrophe isn't imminent?" he asked.

"Not till he's paid off his mortgage." There seemed to be nothing more to say. "I'd best be getting home now."

"I'll help you up."

He put his hands around her waist and lifted her into the saddle. She was light in his arms, and when she looked down to thank him, a smile trembled shyly on her lips. "Thank you, Mr. Robertson," she said.

"You're welcome, Miss Judson."

He opened the gate and she walked Bingo home, her mind alive with romantic conjectures. Mr. Robertson turned and slowly wended his way back to recover his mount. It was foolish of him to be thinking of Miss Judson in amorous terms. She was totally ineligible. He could name offhand half a dozen topnotch heiresses on the catch for him. Some of them were prettier than Mary Anne; all of them had more polish. A man in his position should marry wisely. Long-lashed brown eyes and magical dimples were not a wise choice; they were merely irresistible. The thing to do was to stay away from her, he told himself severely, but somewhere at the back of his mind he was figuring out how he could spare time to see her again.

Chapter Six

Mary Anne entered the house, swollen with importance after her brush with the smugglers, which lost nothing in the telling. Mrs. Plummer was a suitably impressed audience. Her brown eyes bulged from her head, and her face turned pale.

"Glory be to God, it's a miracle you're alive, child. Didn't I warn you not to go out alone? Two of them, and in a nasty shepherd's hut. What a place to have their way with you, as private as may be. You're lucky you weren't raped. I'll lock the doors at once and have Fitch bar up all the broken windows."

"If it weren't for Mr. Robertson, I doubt I'd be alive to tell you the tale, Mrs. Plummer," Mary Anne finished. "Where's Uncle?" One relating of her story only whetted her appetite. She wanted to tell Uncle and Fitch, and she especially wanted to tell Bess Vulch how Mr. Robertson had come dashing to her rescue. What never entered her head was to tell Joseph Horton.

In Lord Edwin's study behind the bolted door, his lordship was in deep conversation with his butler. "The sooner we get it out of here, Fitch, the better," he worried. "It must be done under cover of darkness. I come to think a ship is the safest way. You could sail it up to Folkestone

56

and have the draper pick it up at the dock. He asked if it would be coming by sea or land.''

"My wee boat don't have sails."

"Then you'll have to row the stuff in your fishing smack.''

"Nay, it'd take two trips, and more than two days to row so far and back twice. I could borrow Elroy's fishing boat, but he'd want his cut."

"That no-good Elroy? Can't let him in on it. He's Vulch's man. He'd blow the gaff on us. Could you borrow the boat tonight without telling him?''

"He goes out at night, and we can't move the stuff in daylight.''

Lord Edwin sighed deeply and fell into an unaccustomed fit of poetics. "These are the times that try men's souls, Fitch. The times that try men's souls. I couldn't have said it better myself.''

"It's our minds we should be trying. We need a boat. It can't be impossible here on the coast, where every second shanty has something that floats.''

"You must come up with something and let me know. By tonight, Fitch, at the latest. I'm on nettles with that load just waiting to be discovered and stolen from me.'' His duty done, he went to harry Plummer into serving lunch.

Last night's chicken served cold was a welcome treat from ham and cheese. Mary Anne related her morning's adventure, with much emphasis on Mr. Robertson's heroism.

Her uncle was in such good humor to learn the Frenchies were wasting their time at Christian's shepherd's hut that he forgot his anger with Robertson. "Well done of the lad. I'll thank him next time we meet. One ought always to be civil to the lower classes—show them how a gentleman behaves. *Noblesse oblige*, what?''

Miss Judson felt free to ask if he planned to go into the village that afternoon. He did, but his errand was to sniff around for a boat he might borrow for one night and he didn't want his niece hobbling his progress. "Not today," he lied easily. "I'm going to speak to some workmen about getting the roof fixed, if they'll do it on tick. The plaster in my bedroom has turned brown and wet. It looks like one of Plummer's plum puddings before it goes into the oven. Can't have the ceiling falling on my head."

No trip to Dymchurch, then, no meeting with Mr. Robertson. Mary Anne was disappointed, but not disconsolate. She would do as he had suggested and search the house for the silk. It was a large house, with easy access from outside by any of half a dozen doors that no one bothered to lock at night. The silk might have been stored in the cellar, for instance.

Lord Edwin left immediately after lunch, and Mary Anne was about to begin her search when there was a loud banging on the front door. Mr. Robertson! was the first thing that popped into her head. She went with a trembling smile to admit him and found herself staring at Mr. Codey, the customs man. In his hand he held a document, signed by Judge Endicott and set with his seal.

"I have a warrant to search these premises, Miss Judson," the little fellow stated importantly.

Codey was the very picture of a bantam cock: small, pigeon-breasted, with hair the color of an orange, a beaky nose, and an aggressive expression. He was well known and hated as an avid worker.

"Who had it sworn out?" she asked. "If that wretch of a Vulch . . ."

"It was sworn out by Viscount Dicaire."

"Who the devil is Viscount Dicaire? I never heard of him."

"Some London friend of Vulch," he admitted shamelessly. "A big chief in the customs-and-excise department. After one glance at the paper from Dicaire, Endicott couldn't move his stamp fast enough. I figure the cellar is the likeliest place. Easiest access. I've brought my own torches. Stand aside, if you please, ma'am."

Mary Anne stood aside to let Codey precede her, but she followed him to the kitchen. When Codey had descended, she informed Mrs. Plummer of Vulch's heinous trick.

"Where's my rolling pin?" Mrs. Plummer demanded, eyes blazing. "I know right where it is, if I could only find it. I'll lay it over Codey's red head if he goes smashing the last dozen bottles of wine in the cellar."

"I'll make sure he doesn't," Mary Anne said. She took up a candle to follow Codey into the cellar.

"He'll not find a thing but mice and black beetles," Mrs. Plummer said with grim satisfaction.

He also found a nest of bats, but as a quick scoot through the bowels of the house was enough to show him no large bales of silk were there, he soon returned above stairs.

"Open your pantry, Mrs. Plummer," he commanded.

She strode, arms akimbo and face red with indignation, to throw open the innocent door. "Mind you keep your fingers off that bowl of leftover chicken!" she warned, brandishing her rolling pin. A mouse came running out, and she vented her wrath on it.

Mary Anne was close behind Codey as he peered into pickle bins and behind a wheel of cheese, and in an excess of enthusiasm tapped at walls and floors for a secret passage.

"Mind you don't knock the walls down," Mrs. Plummer called in.

The search continued upstairs and down, through airless parlors and mildewed bedchambers and sodden attics. After two hours, Officer Codey was assured of Lord Edwin's innocence.

"The house is clean," he announced. After a glance at his dusty fingers, he altered this misleading phrase. "That is to say—the silk ain't here. It's tiring work," he said, wiping his brow and looking about for a keg of ale.

"I'd offer you a seat, but all the empty chairs are full," Mrs. Plummer said, grimly placing a dirty pot on the one closest to him.

With a glower and a military straightening of his shoulders, Codey said, "As you were, ladies." Then he saluted and left.

Mrs. Plummer stared at his swaggering departure. "Gudgeon. Why we have to pay taxes to be badgered by the likes of that yellow hammer is above and beyond me. He's set me an hour behind on my work. The bread will have swelled to a mountain." On this complaint she returned to her kitchen.

The untidy condition of the house had been borne in on Miss Judson during the tour, and she went for a dust cloth to tackle the main saloon. "You'd best use beeswax and turpentine, or you'll only rearrange the dust," Mrs. Plummer told her, and supplied these necessities, before returning to beat her bread dough into compliance.

Mary Anne had just tucked a tea towel into her waistband and begun the job of restoring a sheen to ancient furnishings when the door knocker sounded again. This unwonted flurry of visitors was a distraction from her usual solitude, and she quickly whipped off the towel to answer the door. She smiled in surprise to see Mrs. Vulch and her daughter, Bess, standing on her doorstep. Bess was arrayed in yet another new gown. The Vulches were the smartest-looking women in the village, due to their unique closeness to incoming silk.

Fond as they were of silk, however, they did not wear

it during the daytime. Mrs. Vulch was a large, strident, dark-haired woman, florid of complexion and outspoken in the extreme. Bess, having been born into more opulence than her parents, appeared closer to gentility. She wore a fashionable blue and white gown of mulled muslin, with a broad ribbon around the waist. Mary Anne thought the straw cartwheel bonnet must have been sufficient protection from the sun, but it was augmented with a sun umbrella that matched the gown.

Miss Vulch, like most redheads, was prone to spotting from the sun. Even with all her layers of protection, the charge of being bran-faced was not entirely foreign to her. But she did not sink under it. She had pretty brown eyes, a trim figure, a lively manner, and a dowry of ten thousand pounds.

"Mary Anne!" She smiled gaily. "Whatever are you doing with a dust cloth in your hands? My dear, you look a quiz. You have dust on your chin."

"Some ladies don't think it beneath them to pick up a dust cloth, you see," Mrs. Vulch pointed out to her daughter.

"Do come in. I'm delighted you called." Mary Anne smiled and showed them into the Blue Saloon.

Mrs. Vulch perused the chamber closely, trying to figure out why it should be that her own saloon, where everything was bright and new as a penny, failed to achieve the casual air of elegance that still lingered here at the Hall despite the sad disrepair of the chamber. Her piano was as good as new, as no one ever played it. All the books Adrian bought were the same—why, most of the pages weren't even cut.

"You should be out driving on a fine day like this, Mary Anne," Bess said. "I wager that horrid uncle of yours has gone off and left you carriageless. You should make him buy you a phaeton. Papa's buying one for me."

On this breathless rush of words she smiled contentedly around her. Mr. Robertson must have laughed up his sleeve to see such a shambles. She examined the sofa cushion for dirt and brushed it with her gloves before sitting down. Mary Anne had some hopes her friend had come to invite her out for a drive and glanced at the clock to see it was already after three.

"Yes, I would like to go for a drive, but as you said, Uncle is out in the carriage."

"I'd love to take you, but alas, we have dozens of cards to deliver. This one is for you," Bess said, and handed Mary Anne an invitation. "It's only for dinner this evening. Mama thought we ought to do something to entertain Mr. Robertson. You know him, I think?" she asked with a carelessness that was belied by the sparkle in her eyes.

Even delivering cards would have been a welcome diversion, but Miss Vulch didn't offer and Mary Anne disliked to ask. "Yes, I know him," she replied mysteriously.

"You sly dog!" Miss Vulch said. "Don't tell me you've developed a *tendre* for Mr. Robertson. He's only a drapery merchant. Mama said he would not do, didn't you, Mama?"

"Your papa said he would not. He seems very gentlemanly to me."

"He's rather handsome," Bess said forgivingly.

"Rather handsome?" Mary Anne exclaimed. "I would say he's *very* handsome."

"Oh, you *do* like him!" Miss Vulch teased. "Only look at her blush, mama. Joseph will be vexed to hear it. Not that I shall reveal your secret. Wild horses wouldn't drag it from me. Is that the ring Joseph gave you for your birthday?" she asked, having espied the ring. "He dropped by the house last night after leaving you," she added with a quick look from the corner of her eye to see how this went down.

"Yes, Mr. Robertson told me this morning," Mary Anne replied with a very similar look.

She saw a light of avid curiosity on her friend's face. "This morning? Why, how did you come to see Mr. Robertson today? He said he was going out looking for the silk."

"I met him while I was out riding," Mary Anne said, and had the pleasure of telling her story to a new and enthusiastic audience that hung on every word and asked a hundred questions.

"Did he kiss you?" Miss Vulch asked, when the recital was done.

"No! Of course he didn't!"

"Some ladies know how to behave themselves." Mrs. Vulch snorted. "Kissing, indeed! Miss Judson is shocked at you, Bess."

"I swear, I wouldn't put it a pace past him. He's such a flirt. But I can obviously tell *you* nothing of Mr. Robertson," she said, and went on to relate every word that had left his lips and a good many that had not.

"I'm sure I don't know when you had such a cose with him," Mrs. Vulch exclaimed. "Every time I've spotted him, he's dashing letters off to London."

"I would offer you a glass of wine, but you are in a hurry to deliver your cards," Mary Anne mentioned.

"Oh, the party is small. Just Joseph and you and your uncle. Will Lord Edwin come?" Mrs. Vulch asked eagerly.

Mary Anne was not surprised to hear the "dozens" of guests dwindle to three. She was used to her friend's careless way with facts.

Visits between the two houses were common, but the question brought to mind last night's argument. "I'll have to see if he's engaged this evening," Mary Anne prevaricated. "Of course, I cannot accept if Uncle is busy elsewhere with the carriage. I'll have Fitch take our answer as soon as Uncle returns.''

"I hope you can come. Cook is preparing a green goose—your uncle's favorite. And spring lamb,'' Mrs. Vulch tempted.

These enticements were her own effort. She treasured the friendship with Lord Edwin and his niece. The word *parvenu* was unknown to her, but she knew the feeling if she didn't know the word. She had a fine house, a good deal of money, and the best clothes in the village, but she knew her family lacked cachet as surely as she knew Mary Anne and Lord Edwin had it. How the girl grew up so ladylike with no one to guide her was a mystery. It must be something that people were born with, like a squint or gapped teeth.

For half an hour the young ladies discussed fashions and the spring assembly, Miss Vulch's new phaeton, and village gossip, and Mrs. Vulch called her daughter to order from time to time. When at last the Vulches decided Joseph would be home from his day's labor, they rose and took their leave.

"I do hope you can come tonight,'' Mrs. Vulch said.

"Do try,'' Bess added. "I have the sweetest new bonnet I want to show you—glazed straw, with *coquelicot* ribbons. It would look marvelous on you, Mary Anne. Why don't you buy one and we'll pose as twins? Do you think the ribbons will clash with my hair?''

Miss Judson thought *coquelicot* was a bad choice but said she'd give her opinion when she saw the bonnet on.

"If you can't come, I'll give Mr. Robertson your particular apologies.''

"Oh, no! I shouldn't want you to do that!''

"He'll be devastated. How I should like to see Joseph and he sparring for your attentions. It would be better than a drama, wouldn't it, Mama?''

"Better than that wretched piece your papa took us to in London, and that's a fact."

"I thought Joseph would give you an engagement ring for your birthday yesterday," Bess said. "Twenty-fourth, wasn't it?"

"Yes, I'm twenty-four," Mary Anne said, and ignored the other speech, which had been delivered in a quizzing way.

"Mama is having a huge party for my twenty-first, next month. Turtle soup, if you please! Mr. Robertson says it is all the crack in London. Served by all the smarts and swells, from what he hears the customers say in his shop," she said, and took up her sun umbrella. "I feel quite a spinster, still single at such an advanced age."

"Perhaps Joseph will give *you* a ring for your birthday," Mary Anne replied. "I didn't realize he was calling on you till Mr. Robertson mentioned it."

"Calling on me? My dear child, what can you mean? He only came to see the family, as he often does lately. His mother and Mama are becoming bosom bows. I can't imagine what plans they are hatching," she said with an arch smile at her mother, and they finally left.

"Let Miss Judson worry her fine head about *that*," Bess said as they hastened to their carriage.

"You'd do better not to advertise you're after him," her mother cautioned.

It was no secret in the Vulch family that Joseph was becoming interested in Bess, but till his interest firmed, her mother would have preferred to keep it within the family. His mama fostered the affair. Bess's mama connived at it, and between the three of them, they hoped to convince Joseph that ten thousand pounds was better than a load of debt.

Before long Lord Edwin returned, smiling the smile of the wicked. He had found his boat. Jeremy Black was down with the flu and had agreed to let Fitch hire his for the night. It was to be picked up under cover of darkness by Fitch and sailed down to Horton Hall.

Mary Anne didn't remark her uncle's smile. She was too worried that he'd refuse the Vulches' invitation to dinner.

"Take mutton with that smuggler? I hope you sent them home with a flea in their ear," he exclaimed.

"I told them Fitch would deliver your answer. They're having green goose and new spring lamb," she mentioned hopefully.

"Green goose, eh?" he said. "What mess of pottage is Plummer brewing up for us?"

"She made a stew with the leftover chicken."

This wasn't as bad as it could be. Lord Edwin liked Plummer's chicken stew. It was really the bottle of brandy Vulch always served after dinner that turned the trick. For all his common ways, Vulch poured freely.

"I daresay you'd like to go and have a cose with Miss Vulch."

"I always enjoy Bess's company." This wasn't the moment to warn her uncle that Joseph Horton would be of the party.

It would get in the evening pleasantly till it was time to see Fitch off. "Very well, then, you may write up an acceptance for Fitch to deliver."

"Oh, and, Uncle, I forgot to tell you. Codey was here with a search warrant from Lord Dicaire in London. They rooted through the entire house. I think you should write a letter of complaint to the papers."

Lord Edwin looked interested, no more. He liked writing letters of complaint to the journals. This suggestion was given to distract his mind from Vulch's perfidy, which might yet endanger the dinner party. She waited with bated

66

breath to hear what he would say and was surprised to hear a tinny laugh issue from his throat.

"Maybe that will convince the old wether I'm innocent. I wish I had been here to see Codey's face."

"Mrs. Plummer was perfectly uncivil to him, I'm happy to say. Did you convince the roofer to fix the roof on tick?" she remembered to ask.

"Eh? What's that? Oh, the roof. No, he wasn't home. I'll see him tomorrow. No hurry."

Mary Anne happily hastened to the desk to write up the acceptance to the Vulches' dinner party. She had her new shawl to wear. She hadn't thought to mention that to Bess.

Chapter Seven

While his niece arranged her toilette, Lord Edwin went haring off after Fitch to notify him of developments.

"They've been and searched the house," Lord Edwin said, smiling. "That's pretty good evidence they have no idea where the silk is. We should have easy sailing tonight. I'm dining with old Vulture, but shall get away early to give you a hand with the loading."

Fitch was undeceived as to what form the "help" would take. "Nay, stay as late as you like, and sop up a tot of his brandy for me whilst you're there. I'll not be leaving till midnight. I'll load her up while Codey has his nightly draught at the tavern."

"I wish I could go to Folkestone with you, Fitch, but someone must be here in case of trouble at this end. Remember, now, you sleep on the boat and get to McNally's Drapery Shop first thing in the morning to let him know the cargo's in. I'll be over later in the morning to collect payment."

"Aye, aye, Cap'n." Fitch grinned.

Above stairs, Miss Judson decided that while Joseph did not merit her new silk shawl, Mr. Robertson did, especially as he might not still be in Dymchurch to see it at the assembly. She also wore her best blue silk gown and made a very pretty picture as she took stock of herself at her dim mirror before going below. The sight of his niece flaunting the ill-gotten shawl threw Lord Edwin into a pelter when she came down. Very likely Vulch knew the Frenchies' habit of including one worked piece of silk as a sample. To see his niece wrapped in that obviously new shawl would rekindle his suspicions.

"Do you like it, Uncle?" she asked, and made a pirouette to show off the embroidered back of the shawl.

"Licked to a splinter. Very pretty, my dear," he said, but in a strangled voice. Egad, how could he get the thing off her back without raising suspicion? "But you'll want your wrap for the trip, eh? Just carry the shawl and put it on when you arrive."

"It's not that chilly. I'll be fine in the carriage," she replied.

"It smells like a storm brewing, and we're taking the gig," he improvised hastily. "Fitch has some—some work to do while we're away and isn't free to drive us. Since we'll be in the open carriage, I wish you would wear your wrap."

"Couldn't Jem drive us? My hair will be blown to pieces."

"Jem is busy," Lord Edwin said firmly.

"What is Fitch doing?"

"He's hammering some boards up in the attic ceiling. Just get your wrap and let us be off. Give me your shawl. I'll carry it for you."

Mary Anne thought she would be warm enough in the gig, but to protect her toilette from dust, she agreed to wear her wrap. Her uncle removed the shawl and sent her upstairs. "I'll be awaiting you in the gig," he called after her. Then he took the shawl into the saloon and hid it under the sofa cushions.

She was desolate to discover, when they reached

Vulches', that Uncle had forgotten the shawl at home. But the delightful accents of Mr. Robertson coming from the saloon soon put it out of her mind. She went on trembling knees to make her curtsy to the assembled crowd. She noticed that Bess was at Mr. Robertson's elbow. That, she thought, must account for Joseph's having added himself to the other end of the sofa. There he sat, guarding the heiress, as wary as a dog at his meal. Mr. Robertson sat between them. He rose when she entered. Joseph and Mr. Vulch rose, too.

As soon as the greetings were over, Bess invited Mary Anne to sit on the chair closest to her. In a carrying voice she said, "I've been waiting this age for you! I'm so happy you could come. Doesn't she look lovely, Mr. Robertson? I see what has been detaining you, Mary Anne—your toilette." Her head turned from one to the other at these playful sallies.

"I meant to wear a new shawl I got for my birthday," Mary Anne said.

"You wanted to put me in the shade, sly wretch! Never mind, I'm sure your old shawl is enough to eclipse me entirely." She gave Joseph a glance from the corner of her eye but heard no denial of this statement. "I knew you would make a special effort when I told you who would be here," she said with a meaningful nod of her head in Mr. Robertson's direction. Behind her fingers, but in a perfectly carrying voice, she added, "You see, I have saved you a chair beside him." The speech was accompanied by a knowing smirk and a quick dart of her eyes toward Mr. Robertson.

Next she turned her full attention to him and said in the same stage whisper, "Didn't I tell you she would be here, James? But you mustn't take the compliment wholly to yourself. Joseph is also an attraction. I expect to see you both with daggers drawn over Miss Judson before the night is out."

Mary Anne noted with interest that Mr. Robertson's name was James, and Bess, the bold creature, was making free of it already.

Mr. Robertson hardly knew how to reply to this artless performance. He bowed and smiled, and said he feared they were in for rain.

"I fear so," Miss Judson agreed, "and we came in the gig, too."

"Speaking of rigs," Joseph said, pitching his words across Bess to Robertson, "that is a mighty fine curricle you're driving, Mr. Robertson. Sixteen miles an hour, I fancy?"

"Fifteen at least, on a good open stretch of road," Mr. Robertson replied.

"Ho, with that pair of grays, I fancy seventeen or eighteen isn't above them. They have got Alvanley's beat."

"Actually they are Alvanley's old team. He sold them to me last winter," Mr. Robertson said.

"By Jove!" Joseph smiled. "I expect you're a member of the F.H.C. With that team, you could pass anything on the road."

"No, the Four-in-Hand Club decrees that the pace must not exceed a trot. Passing another coach on the road is prohibited. The driving is very carefully regulated."

"I should think so!" Joseph said. "I have seen you fellows assemble at Hanover Square for your dart to Salt Hill. They say your dinners at the Windmill are a regular brawl."

"Only port wine is served," Mr. Robertson said. "We *do* have to drive back as well, you know."

"Exactly!" Joseph nodded.

"So you are a notable whip, James, and a model of

sobriety. I trust a certain someone is taking notes of all this," Bess said, directing her words toward Miss Judson.

When Joseph leaned forward to resume the conversation, Bess took him by the arm and restrained him. "We must be discreet, Joseph," she said playfully. "Privacy— that is what they will want. I'm sure they wish us both at Jericho."

Certainly Mary Anne wished one of them there. Bess was impossible, but Joseph's behavior was equally strange. It seemed he was buttering Mr. Robertson up very lavishly. Why was he at such pains to ingratiate a drapery merchant? She cast a puzzled frown at Mr. Robertson.

"You didn't bring a pen!" he accused playfully. "Never mind, I'll have a judge write up my character and post it down to you. I trust you are also a fan of the F.H.C.?"

"I haven't the least notion what you're talking about," she said, blinking.

"That doesn't stop Joseph from agreeing with me," he murmured with an ironic flicker of his eyes toward that gentleman.

Mary Anne chastened his irony with a blank stare. "F.H.C.—it sounds like a government commission."

"And you, Miss Judson, sound like my maiden aunts. A lady is always deaf to a gentleman's solecisms. Very well, we shall discuss governmental ABC's, if you wish. Agencies, boards, and commissions, the letters stand for, at Whitehall."

"How do you know that? What dealings do *you* have at Whitehall?"

"Though a lowly merchant, I am allowed to sit in the visitors' gallery and watch the elite squander my tax money," he answered with an easy smile that concealed his gaffe.

Mrs. Vulch nodded contentedly to see how clever her daughter was growing and what a gossoon Miss Judson was, throwing her bonnet at a drapery merchant while an excellent parti went to waste. Amazing how the girl could turn out looking half-decent in that old gown that might have been rescued from Noah's ark.

To cement the partners, she had dinner called five minutes early and made sure to seat Miss Judson away from Joseph, beside Mr. Robertson. Mrs. Vulch's frequent admonitions to her daughter not to talk across the table were not entirely obeyed, but the distance severely limited Mr. Robertson's access to Bess.

"I see you've recovered from the morning's excitement," Mr. Robertson said to Mary Anne.

"I'm feeling much better," she admitted.

"And looking admirable. What is your excuse for not being at Dymchurch at two this afternoon?" he asked. "Before you contrive some wildly improbably tale, I must warn you, Bess told me of her visit. You were at home, miss, taking a dust cloth to the furniture! Had you been in hands with your modiste or coiffeur, I could understand, but I assure you I'm not used to playing second fiddle to a dust cloth."

It was hard to be angry with Bess for relaying the menial nature of her afternoon's occupation when Mr. Robertson smiled so charmingly. "Uncle had the carriage out, and he doesn't like me to drive into Dymchurch alone in the gig," she explained.

"Uncles can be a sad trial, but in this case, I'm bound to say I agree with Lord Edwin. I'm happy to see the little argument the other evening was a tempest in a teapot. I made sure your uncle wouldn't accept the Vulches' invitation this evening."

"Well," she confided, "we were only having chicken stew at home, and besides, Uncle's all out of brandy."

Mr. Robertson hid the unsteadiness of his lips with his

fork. "Then it wasn't just the lure of being teased by Bess and the presence of Joseph Horton that drew you hither?"

"No." She scowled and promptly changed the subject. "Have you had any luck in finding your silk, Mr. Robertson?" she asked.

"Not directly, but I could tell you ten or a dozen places where it is *not* hidden, which is a sort of negative success, if one is an optimist. It limits the places it could be."

"You can positively strike Horton Hall off your list as well. We had a visit from Codey this afternoon. He went through the house with a fine-tooth comb. Vulch used his connections with Whitehall to get a search warrant. A Lord Dicaire obliged him."

Mr. Robertson was well aware of the visit and made some commiserating remarks about the nuisance of customs men. "I hope whoever took it has got it stored in a dry place. That sky looked as if it was brewing up a good storm."

"How long can you afford to keep looking for the cargo, Mr. Robertson?" she asked. Her hope was to discover whether he would be in town for the assembly.

"There's no point returning to London without it. My shelves are empty."

"But shouldn't you be trying to secure another cargo? There are dozens of smugglers here on the cost who might oblige you."

"That, of course, is why I'm remaining for a few days. I'm making contact with other importers. You sound remarkably eager to be rid of me, ma'am."

"That was not my meaning!" she exclaimed, chagrined to be so misunderstood till she saw the secret light of laughter in his eyes.

"I feel half the town would relish the sight of my back. Your Joseph has already wondered aloud two or three times why I linger so long. Mrs. Vulch fears I have designs on

74

her well-dowered daughter. And, of course, Lord Edwin has invited me in no uncertain terms to depart his house. Once Vulch becomes tired of my phiz, I shall have no recourse but to pay for my rack and manger at the inn."

"I shouldn't think Mr. Vulch would treat a good customer so shabbily," she told him.

"I figure he'll tolerate me for another twenty-four hours. You might be interested to know the French smugglers are returning to France this evening. Vulch was instrumental in getting their lugger freed from customs."

"Vulch?" she asked. "He wouldn't have that much clout. It was no doubt Lord Dicaire."

"Perhaps he was instrumental. Their leaving means, in case you wonder why I mention it to you, that you should be able to take your usual ride tomorrow morning without fear of being molested. Do you usually ride around ten o'clock?"

Mary Anne knew from his questioning smile that it was an invitation to meet him. "Yes, if the weather holds up."

"I, too, am in the habit of taking my constitutional at that hour. Shall we make it your uncle's meadow?"

"You can come to the house, Mr. Robertson. I don't like to sneak behind my uncle's back. I assure you, it isn't necessary."

He cleared his throat and glanced along the table to Lord Edwin. "There is the little matter of my being hinted away," he mentioned.

"It wasn't you he was angry with. He and Vulch have ring-round fights, but they're really very good friends."

From along the table, Lord Edwin was heard to exclaim, "Rubbish!" and they both looked to hear what new argument had arisen.

"You see," Mrs. Vulch told him, "that *was* a clap of thunder just now."

As though to confirm her assertion, another roll of thun-

75

der reverberated in the heavens, and a flash of lightning was seen beyond the window, but why should this far-from-unusual occurrence send Lord Edwin into an apoplexy?

"I'd rather have it at night than destroying the day. At least it shan't keep us from shopping," Mrs. Vulch said unconcernedly, and lifted her fork. The spring lamb was delicious.

"We came in the gig," Mary Anne said, feeling this was why Uncle was upset.

The lovely spring lamb went untasted by Lord Edwin, though not uneaten. Now, how the deuce was Fitch to get the cargo loaded and delivered to Folkestone in the teeth of a howling storm? The stuff would be worthless if it got wet, and a wrapping of oilskin paper couldn't protect it from this downpour.

Mr. Robertson noticed the man's agitation. "I'll be happy to drive you home if it is the open carriage that worries you."

"But your curricle is open, too, Mr. Robertson," Bess reminded him. "Joseph will be driving right past the door. I'm sure he'll be happy to deliver them home."

Mrs. Vulch shot a killing glance across the table. "Your papa will provide for his guests' comfort, Bess," she said in a voice like vinegar.

Toward the end of dinner there was a hiatus in the bad weather. The storm wasn't over, but Lord Edwin felt if he and his niece left at once, they'd get home before the skies opened again. With a longing look at the brandy decanter sitting on the sideboard with the port, he excused himself and his niece and said they would dart back to the Hall at once.

Mr. Robertson soon said his good-nights and went upstairs, and Mrs. Vulch had the satisfaction of seeing Joseph Horton settle in by the grate with Bess for a hand of cards. She removed her husband to the far corner of the room to allow the young couple some privacy.

"I don't know why you were in such a hurry to leave," Mary Anne scolded as they drove through the night, with the trees under which they drove showering them quite as thoroughly as actual rain would do. "We seldom get invited out to dinner, Uncle. Why didn't you accept Mrs. Vulch's offer of a drive home in their carriage?"

"It's my attics I'm worried about," he told her, but she knew well enough that the sodden attics hadn't concerned him during all the years they had been leaking. Why now?

He let her off at the door, and she scampered in while he took the gig around to the stable. Mrs. Plummer met her at the door. "You're back early! Did your uncle and Vulch come to blows again?"

"No, Uncle was in a great yank to get home while the rain had let up. I don't know why Fitch couldn't have driven us."

"You left your shawl behind," she said.

"Uncle left it behind."

"What did he hide it under the sofa cushions for? Lucky I happened to see the fringe hanging out and rescued it before it was a parcel of wrinkles."

"Hid it? Why would he do that?"

"I haven't a notion. He's acting queerly of late. And Fitch is as bad. He's gone and hired Jeremy Black's boat. It's sitting down at the dock, partly hidden in the reeds. I was at the window looking at the lightning and happened to see him pulling in. It gave me a turn. I thought it was the Frenchies, and I here alone."

"The Frenchies have gone home. Vulch arranged to get their lugger freed. No doubt his friend Lord Dicaire gave him a hand. But what would Fitch want with the boat? He couldn't plan to go fishing on a night like this."

"They're up to something," Mrs. Plummer scolded.

"I suspected as much when Uncle darted home without even having a glass of brandy. Where's Fitch now?"

"He didn't come in at all. He seems to be loading the hay from the old haywain onto that boat he borrowed."

Mary Anne blinked. "What?"

"I only got the odd glimpse through the window when the lightning flashed, but it looked as if he was putting hay onto the boat."

"That's ridiculous."

"Wet hay at that. Oh, there's something odd afoot here, missie, and I mean to find out what it is as soon as ever Fitch comes in."

They went to the window and stared through the shadows down to the shore. With no moon, visibility was nearly nonexistent, but they thought they saw some movement in the rushes.

"I'm going to put on some older clothes and see what he's up to," Mary Anne decided.

"Why don't you wait and ask your uncle when he comes in?"

"Because he won't come in, and wouldn't tell the truth if he did. He'll join Fitch. This has something to do with his eagerness to get home. And he nearly choked on the lamb when Mrs. Vulch was talking about the storm," she added as she ran toward the stairs.

She threw her silk shawl on the bed. It called up a memory of that rather peculiar trip to Folkestone, with Uncle talking to all the drapers in their private offices. He'd bought the shawl at Folkestone, but he'd visited plenty of other shops after that. You didn't have a private conference only to discuss the purchase of a length of silk, which had been his excuse.

She disliked to acknowledge, even to herself, what she was thinking. The cargo of silk abandoned at their doorstep. Uncle's rare good humor the next morning. He *had* stolen the silk! While Codey searched the stables and icehouse and barn and house, the silk had sat under the load of hay on the old hay wain. And now Uncle had hired this boat to take it away and sell it to one of the merchants he had visited. Good God, if he was caught, he'd hang.

That's why Fitch had brought Jeremy Black's boat here and why Uncle had been on the fidgets when he learned about the storm. Almost before she had digested this dreadful idea, the image of Mr. Robertson cropped into her head. What would he think to learn her uncle was a thief? She must keep it from him.

She was correct in assuming Uncle wouldn't come to the house. Lord Edwin didn't even stable the gig. He drove it down to the shore to consult with Fitch.

By the time he got there, Fitch had loaded the cargo and was on the lookout for his employer. A strong wind had come up, and before long a regular deluge was pouring down on them.

"I daren't tackle the trip in this gale," Fitch warned.

"Rubbish. You'll make it with no trouble. Is the stuff safe? You have it in the hold?"

"She's high and dry, but she won't be if I take the boat out tonight."

"Use your head, man. You can't wait till morning. Codey is on the qui vive. He even searched the Hall this afternoon."

"Aye, I'm thinking the Hall is as safe a place as any, seeing as how it's already been searched. We could stash the goods for a week or so till the excitement calms down," Fitch suggested, and looked to see how this idea was greeted.

"If they take it into their heads to come back and I'm caught with the goods under my very roof, I'm done for,

Fitch. A fox in a chicken coop would look innocent beside me. You'll have to think of something else."

"There's the stables. Anyone could hide it there. It's no proof *we* had anything to do with it."

"There's too much traffic in the stables. People coming and going. The old barn, perhaps . . . the hayloft, and we take away the ladder to discourage anyone from going up."

"It's heavy work, hauling the bales up the ladder. I've already loaded them once tonight and will have to unload them and take them to the barn."

"Use the gig. Just get the bales into the barn tonight, and you can take them aloft in the morning. I don't want you to strain yourself, Fitch. Take it easy. Use the gig, and mind you put it away right and tight when you're finished. Better finish the job early in the morning. Say, five o'clock."

Happy with his contribution, Lord Edwin turned to leave.

"I'll have to take the boat back, too, after I've unloaded her. I doubt I'll be finished by five."

"I told you," Lord Edwin said, "use the gig."

But the gig wouldn't wade through the water and lift the hundred bales into itself and unload them again at the barn. Fitch foresaw a hard night's work.

"And mind you cover the stuff well in the barn for tonight. There's no saying Codey won't be snooping around."

Lord Edwin went darting through the rain to the Hall and walked in to be met by two glaring females.

"Well, Uncle, you have some explaining to do!" Mary Anne charged.

Chapter Eight

"But, Uncle, it's *stealing*!" Mary Anne exclaimed, horrified, after Lord Edwin had been browbeaten into a confession. "You'll be tried and hanged."

"Drawn and quartered." Plummer nodded severely.

"Only if I get caught, which I shan't. They've already searched my premises twice. That should convince Codey I'm innocent. The nerve of him, accusing me of thievery!" He still bristled with indignation to consider this iniquity. "I shall write that letter to the journals as you suggested, Mary Anne. That was doing it pretty brown, entering and searching my house behind my back."

"The stuff is in the barn now, you say?" she asked.

"It soon will be, if that lazy hound of a Fitch isn't asleep on the job. I told him to put it in the hayloft and take away the ladder, but he said he would be too tired. Tired, and all he has to do is put it in the gig. It's Dobbin who will be tired, after jogging us down to Vulches' and back."

"Mighty thoughtful of you," Mrs. Plummer said grimly. "I didn't hear a word of this. I'm deaf and dumb, if they go asking me any questions. I'm going to make Fitch a pot of coffee. The poor lad must be frozen stiff as my sheets in winter."

"An excellent notion, Plummer. Bring me a pot to my office. I have some ciphering to do," Lord Edwin said, and left, rubbing his hands in satisfaction.

Mrs. Plummer gave an annoyed *tsk*. "There goes the most selfish beast in nature."

Mary Anne went to the kitchen with Mrs. Plummer to discuss the affair. "Are we accessories, Mrs. Plummer?" she worried.

"Not I; I know nothing about it. I suggest you turn deaf and blind as well, missie."

"If Uncle insists on being a thief, I wish he would just sell the stuff to Mr. Robertson and have done with it. I don't think Mr. Robertson would ask too many questions. He's very eager to get some silk, for his shelves are empty."

When the coffee was made, Mary Anne offered to deliver it to Fitch. "I'll take a cup up to Uncle first and try to persuade him to return the stuff to Vulch," she said.

"Your uncle's as stubborn as he is crooked. Let him sell it to Mr. Robertson and have done with it."

It was true; there was no dissuading Uncle when he had made up his mind. But she must at least keep him out of jail, and she came up with an idea.

"You could store it in Mr. Christian's shepherd hut and have Fitch take the payment. In that way you wouldn't be directly involved," she outlined to Lord Edwin.

"Everybody knows Fitch is my man. You might as well put a notice in the papers. In Folkestone I called myself Mr. Smith," Lord Edwin added, and smiled at his cleverness.

"Fitch could wear a mask," she suggested. "There's no saying Jeremy Black will let Fitch have his boat another night, you know. And the trip to Folkestone is dangerous. The customs men are out along the coast all the time."

Lord Edwin's fingers played along his cheek. "There's

something in that," he said. "Perhaps I should tell Fitch to take it along to Christian's hut tonight."

With a thought to the assembly on Saturday, Mary Anne objected. "It might be better to make sure Codey has already searched Christian's hut. It would be a pity if Fitch took it there, then Codey decided to search it."

Her uncle was astonished at her cleverness. "By the living jingo, I come to think I should have had you in on it from the start. You're right; I shall write an anonymous note off to Codey telling him the stuff is at Christian's hut, and *after* he searches it, I'll have Fitch put the cargo there tomorrow, say, around ten in the morning."

But if Mr. Robertson got his cargo in the morning, he might leave town before the assembly that night. "I think you should wait a day before transferring the silk to Christian's hut, Uncle," she said cautiously. "Just to be on the safe side, you know. Meanwhile, it will be quite safe in the hayloft, since that's already been searched."

"I'll have Fitch snoop around Christian's place and see if Codey takes any interest after he finds it empty. If the coast is clear, there's no point dallying. The sooner it's over, the sooner I get my money. And there will be a little bonus in it for you, too, missie."

"No! I don't want anything to do with stolen goods!"

Lord Edwin stared at her foolishness. "Stolen from the Frenchies! That isn't stealing; it's patriotism. Vulch didn't pay for the cargo. I checked with him tonight. 'Old Albert Menard is out his blunt,' he told me, and laughed. In times of war, you know," he added piously, "it is every Englishman's duty to bilk the Frenchies out of all we can. The money would only go to buy bullets for Boney." On this piece of rationalization, he lifted the coffee cup and sipped daintily, wishing he had a tot of brandy to put in it.

He took up the pen and began his note to Codey and

the letter to the journal. Mary Anne carried all the weight of worry and guilt that her uncle seemed to ignore. But she was happy to know Uncle was only stealing from the Frenchies. That would be a good point to make if he ended up in the dock. She put on her wrap and took the coffee down to Fitch.

The night air was heavy with fog and drizzle. Through the cloudlike mist she heard the heavy clip-clop of hooves and the jingle of the harness. She soon saw the gig lumbering up from the shore, heavily weighted with its cargo of silk. Fitch was hunched over the reins, urging the nag on to a faster pace. He jerked to attention when he discerned her.

"Oh, 'tis you, Miss Judson!" he exclaimed. "I'm just—just—"

"I know all about it, Fitch," she said severely, and handed him the jug of coffee. "You and Uncle should be ashamed of yourselves."

"Ashamed! Why, it's an act of patriotism."

"I know all about your patriotism, too," she said, and accepted a hand up into the gig. She told Fitch about the plan to put the stuff in Christian's hut and sell it to Mr. Robertson.

"A mask, eh?" He smiled, rather pleased with this piece of melodrama. "You don't think Robertson would turn nasty? I mean to say, if he knows we stole the stuff, he might take it into his noggin not to pay. Plummer tells me he had a pistol when he rescued you from the Frenchies. I don't have a pistol—not one that works." Nothing "worked" at Horton Hall, including the master.

"He's a businessman. He doesn't care who he buys his silk from. He'll pay, never fear."

"But it was odd he carried a pistol," Fitch said.

"Yes, that *was* odd," she agreed, frowning into the shadows.

Why would a drapery merchant travel with a pistol? And, really, Mr. Robertson hadn't at all the air of a merchant. He was very elegant, with that ease of manners more usually encountered amongst the ton. She had always thought it odd he had come racing after his silk so early, too, almost before it had time to arrive in London. Did all merchants take so active a part in the delivery of their goods? He had been out searching the neighborhood when she met him at the shepherd's hut.

Was it possible Mr. Robertson was something other than what he let on? But who could he be? The only other class interested in smuggling was customs men. Good God, was he a customs man sent to the coast to catch the smugglers? He had even put out notice of a ten percent reward, and that was an old customs trick. She remembered, too, that he had not only carried a pistol but had spoken French like a native. Was he perhaps a Frenchman in disguise— perhaps the leader of the party who had abandoned the ship? He might have been hiding out at the hut to try to capture the thief—her uncle!

"Oh, dear," she said in a weak voice. "Stop the horse, Fitch. I must speak to Uncle!"

Fitch drew to a halt and she hopped down. She raced toward the Hall, her mind in turmoil at the awful imbroglio she had nearly thrown her uncle into. A minor worry was soon added to her heavier fears. The sodden grass was making a mess of her evening slippers, and with the spring assembly looming, she must preserve them. She'd have drier walking if she went home under the trees that sheltered the west side of the Hall and entered by the back door.

She flew toward the row of beeches and scampered along, congratulating herself on this idea. The leaves were so thick, the ground under them was still dry after that downpour. It was as she made the dart toward the protection of the last tree that she heard it—the telltale clink of a harness and whickering of a horse. As she entered the dry darkness of the tree's canopy, she nearly fell against a warm flank. The nag, in its surprise, emitted a louder sound than before.

Her first instinctive thought was that Fitch had used Uncle's mount and forgotten to stable it afterward. With so many things on his mind, it was no wonder. She patted the horse and began feeling for the rope to untie it. Her fingers encountered hide as smooth as silk and the firm hindquarters of a horse in the prime of life, which Uncle's nag hadn't been for a decade. Almost at the same moment she realized there was a second horse tethered on the other side of the tree.

Codey! was her first awful fear. But Codey rode a rusty old cob not much better than Uncle's Bingo, and he rode alone. No one in the neighborhood had such bloods as this except Vulch. The sneak had ridden over in the dark of night to have another look for the silk. Poltroon that he was, he'd been afraid to come alone. He had one of his grooms or footmen with him. Vulch instilled no terror in Miss Judson's breast. The only emotion there was hot anger.

She strode out from the concealment of the tree and headed for the stable, certain that was where he was searching. As she drew nearer, she even saw the erratic movement of a rush light through the gaping boards of the building. With no effort at silence, she threw open the door and called in the direction of the light, "Well, Mr. Vulch, can I do something for you?"

It seemed, in the moment the light remained lit, that a dozen men suddenly jumped out at her, though she actually remembered only three distinctly. Two of them came from the unused loose boxes, and they were horrid, rough-looking men she didn't recognize. In the hand of one she

86

glimpsed a hoe; the other held a pistol. The only gentleman in the group was not Mr. Vulch but Mr. Robertson. He looked as startled to see her as the others did. He was the one holding the rush light. Its reflection burned in his eyes, giving him the aspect of a demon.

His mouth opened in silent astonishment. That was the last thing she saw before the rush light was whipped out of his hand and extinguished. In the pitch black of the barn she was suddenly shoved aside. There was a flurry of activity and a mumble of muted words as the intruders pelted out of the barn to disappear into the night. She stood gasping in fright as the horses under the beech tree were untied and the men clattered away.

Mary Anne's heart pounded like a drum at the back of her throat. She stood trembling, too frightened to move. Who were those men? As rationality returned, she moved to the door, gathering fortitude to bolt for the house. She listened a moment to be sure they were gone, then tiptoed to the door. She was about to leave when a moan came from the bowels of the stable. Oh, God! One of them was still there, and he was hurt—or playacting to lure her in. She flew out the door and ran pell-mell into a wall of human flesh.

"What's afoot?" Fitch demanded. "I heard the clatter of horses from the barn. Are you all right, Miss Judson?"

"Fitch!" she gasped. "There's someone in the stable. He's wounded, I think."

There was a sound of a body stirring in the shadows. With Fitch there to protect her, Mary Anne had lost her fear. "Who is it?" she called bravely.

A man stumbled into the dim visibility of the doorway, clutching his hand to his head.

"It's Robertson!" Fitch exclaimed, and gave Mary Anne a warning glance.

She saw the look and knew she should heed it, but to

87

see Mr. Robertson with what looked like blood trickling down his forehead caused reason to flee. "James, are you all right?" she demanded, and hurried forward to help him. The "James" popped out unnoticed by her.

He steadied himself with an arm on her shoulder and shook his head. "I may live," he muttered. "Lucky it was only my hard head they smashed."

"Help me get him into the house, Fitch!" she ordered, and with Fitch propping him up on one side, Mary Anne on the other, they hobbled to the kitchen door. Mrs. Plummer had retired for the night. She overheard the fracas from behind her bedroom door, which was adjacent to her kitchen. She got out of bed and put her ear to the door.

"Light the lamp," Mary Anne said. When it was lit, she said, "Here, seat him at the table. Shall I send for a doctor, Mr. Robertson?" she asked, examining his head. What had looked like blood in the darkness proved to be only a lock of wet hair that had fallen forward. The bruise, a sizable one, was on the back of his head.

"That won't be necessary," Mr. Robertson decided, after tenderly feeling his bump.

Mary Anne became aware that Fitch was wildly gesturing and followed him outside the door for a private word.

"I can't abandon my work," he whispered. "I recognized Jed Parker as he pelted off. It was Vulch's men in the stable, looking for the stuff."

"Oh, dear. Do you think they've gone to the barn?"

"Nay, they've left entirely. They went off by the pasture. They must have searched the barn before they came here. That was lucky. I'll get back and finish the job. Are you all right with Robertson?"

"I'll be all right. You run along, Fitch, and take a sharp look around to make sure they haven't come back."

"You'd best warn your uncle what's afoot," Fitch said, and left.

Mary Anne wanted to discover just exactly what Mr. Robertson had been doing and, if possible, who he was, before taking him to her uncle. She sensed that it would best be done in private, for Uncle had a way of diverting conversation to fruitless byways.

"Let me get a cold compress for your head, Mr. Robertson," she said when she returned. "Mrs. Plummer keeps a block of ice in the pantry. I'll chop off some splinters and put them in a towel."

Mr. Robertson had recovered enough to object. "That won't be necessary, but a glass of wine wouldn't go amiss. And, by the by, my name is still James," he added with one of his charmingly intimate smiles. "As I have rescued you, and you have returned the favor by rescuing me, it's time you and I may dispense with the formalities, *n'est-ce pas*?"

All the good of his charming smile was undone by that suggestion, which caused her to narrow her eyes at him. "I always like to repay favors, Mr. Robertson. I expect there is some good reason why you were in my uncle's stable just now."

"My reason can't be unknown to you. I'm still after the silk. I know—your uncle doesn't have it," he said, lifting his hands to fend off her objections. "But someone does, and I still maintain that it didn't get far from where it was first unloaded—at Horton Hall. Vulch's men apparently feel the same way."

"Why did they attack you, if you were working with them?"

"I wasn't working *with* them. They're certainly professional—I hadn't a notion they were in the stable. They must have been there when I arrived. I didn't hear as much as a breath out of either of them. I expect they only meant to stun me and escape. Perhaps they feared your presence would throw me into a fit of gallantry and I'd try to stop

89

them. Or perhaps they didn't recognize me. We haven't been introduced," he added.

"But you recognized them."

"Oh, no! Deduction leads me to conclude who they were, as the French smugglers have already left. The other party interested in recovering the stuff is Vulch. Did you recognize them?"

"No, but Fitch said they were Vulch's men."

"That would be the amiable giant who helped you?"

"Yes, he's our butler—footman—factotum," she said, trying to find a word to cover Fitch's comprehensive duties at the Hall.

Mr. Robertson's intelligent eyes regarded her closely. "He arrived opportunely. What was he doing out on such a night?"

Mary Anne fluffed her wet hair and answered, "Probably looking for the silk, like everyone else. Your reward is a strong incentive."

"Apparently not strong enough. It hasn't produced any results. Er, were *you* also working for the reward, Mary Anne?" A flush warmed her cheeks, whether it was his question that caused it or his brash use of her Christian name, he wasn't sure, but he knew it was demmed attractive.

Mary Anne removed her damp wrap and bustled about the kitchen for wine. Mrs. Plummer kept a few bottles in the pantry to save trips to the cellar. She brought a bottle out and struggled with the cork while thinking of a plausible answer.

"Uncle asked me to check out his mount," she said. "Fitch has so many duties that I occasionally feed the horses."

"At this hour of the night?"

"I was just going to put a blanket over his mount. Bingo's getting old, poor old thing. The damp bothers her."

"The jade your rode this morning? Breathing bothers her, I should think."

She poured two glasses of wine and handed Mr. Robertson one. He lifted the glass in a toast. "To prevarication," he said with a mischievous smile, and drank.

"Yours or mine, Mr. Robertson?" she asked, and sipped her wine, watching him over the rim of her glass.

Only her eyes were visible. Mr. Robertson noticed that they were as big as saucers and as bright as stars. He had always thought he preferred blue eyes but decided that brown eyes were warmer, more alluring. He didn't answer for a moment.

"How did you know I told the Vulches I was going to retire?" he asked, and smiled uneasily.

"That wasn't the prevarication I was referring to."

"Ah!"

She waited, but he said no more. "I think there's more going on here than a mere misplaced cargo of silk. Mr. Vulch intimated as much the first night he came here with you."

Mr. Robertson stirred restively in his chair but said nothing.

"And besides, you wouldn't have left London and come pelting down to Dymchurch before the cargo had time to reach London if empty shelves were your only concern."

"I don't quite grasp the import of all this."

"Neither do I," she admitted. "Your offering a reward indicates you're a customs officer, but that can't be it. If all you wanted to do was catch Vulch, you'd just sit tight and wait for his next cargo." Mr. Robertson gave a vestigial sigh of relief.

"So, why are you here?" she demanded. "You don't look like a drapery merchant. At least not like the local drapers. That jacket is top of the trees."

"Thank you. *I* like it."

She glared. "Joseph wouldn't be trying to to curry favor with you, and you wouldn't be sneering at Bess's forward manners if you were—oh, you know what I mean," she scolded as his smile stretched to a grin.

"I hope I haven't sneered at my hostess's daughter! That would be rag manners, indeed."

"Or even French manners?" she asked archly. "A French phrase trips easily from your tongue, sir."

"*Mais pourquoi pas*? The ton—my customers—speak it!" he explained. She acknowledged that Mr. Robertson didn't look at all French.

"Vulch said there was more involved here than a missing cargo of silk. What did he mean by that? I noticed you gave him a quelling look and he shut up on the spot."

"You don't miss much!"

"That isn't an answer, Mr. Robertson."

"I wish you would sit down. My elegant draper's manners dislike to remain seated while you pace, but if I stand, I'm afraid my head will fall apart."

Mary Anne sat across the table from him and studied him closely. "That isn't an answer, either." She read the indecision on his mobile face and leaned forward eagerly, hoping to hear some exciting explanation of his true identity. Even as she looked, his expression changed. It was as though a shutter had closed, blocking her out.

"The only reason I'm here is to recover that cargo," he said firmly. "There is more to it than silk, but all I'm after is the cargo, and that's all I can tell you. But I will add this, Miss Judson; it is highly dangerous to interfere with me. I won't hesitate to maim or kill, if necessary, to recover it."

A chill settled about her heart. Was this implacable mask the same face that had smiled charmingly at her a moment ago? She didn't doubt for a moment he meant exactly what he said, and her blood turned to wax to think of what might happen to her uncle.

His voice cut into the silence like a saber. "Where is it?" he demanded.

Mary Anne swallowed and set her glass on the table. "I haven't the faintest idea. I haven't seen it."

"You lie very badly. I would like to think it's because you have so little experience at it. I will recover my cargo, Miss Judson, and—"

Mrs. Plummer could take no more. She wrenched the door open and strode boldly into the room. Her head was covered by a mobcap, and a long tail of braid tumbl[ed] down her back. A flannelette robe covered her nightie, [and] below, a pair of flopping mules robbed her of some [dig]nity, but the fire in her eyes more than compensated [for] her toilette.

"Who do you think you're calling a liar? I'll thank you to keep a civil tongue in your head in my kitchen, sir! Maim and kill, is it?" she demanded, and brandished the bread knife she kept by her bedside since the perils of stolen silk were visited on the parish. "If there's an obituary notice, it'll be your own," she warned.

Mr. Robertson rose and gave Mrs. Plummer a bor[ed] look. "I'll speak to Lord Edwin now, if you please, M[iss] Judson," he said.

Mary Anne wanted a private word with her uncle first. There would have to be a radical change of plans. With maiming and killing to be dealt with, he must be very certain to put himself at a distance from the transaction. But unloading the silk became more attractive every minute. There obviously wouldn't be a moment's peace till Mr. Robertson got what he came for.

"I believe he's retired," she said loftily, "but if you'll just wait a moment, I'll see if I can rouse him."

She ran up the back stairs and went flying into Lord

Edwin's study. He was sitting at his desk, smiling over the letters just written. He was particularly pleased with the sheet of invective regarding Codey's harassing of decent, law-abiding citizens.

"Ah, missie, it's you. Listen to this. . . ."

She batted the letter aside. "Robertson's in the kitchen. He wants to see you. And, Uncle, he's talking about maiming and killing to get his silk! Vulch's men were in the stable. . . ."

"Not the barn! They didn't catch Fitch!"

"No. Don't mention Christian's hut till we have a chance to talk. We might want to change the plan."

The door was pushed open. A glacial face stared at them, and Mr. Robertson said, "What plan would that be, Miss Judson?"

Chapter Nine

Lord Edwin always felt he worked best under pressure. Had life permitted him more pressures, he was sure he could have been a hero. He picked up his letter and waved it toward Mr. Robertson.

"My plan of castigating Officer Codey," he said urbanely. "Can't have the likes of that jackanapes running tame through a man's house behind his back. He searched me while I was busy elsewhere, you know. Nice of you to drop by, Mr. Robertson. I haven't thanked you for rescuing this niece of mine. Well done!" That last was an inspired touch. The sort of grace note Wellington would have added.

Mr. Robertson ignored his simple urbanity. "I'm here about the silk, Lord Edwin."

"So was Codey. I think I mentioned his visit? We haven't seen the stuff. Pity. I could use that reward."

Watching the exchange, Mary Anne was very glad Mr. Robertson was unaware of her uncle's telltale habit of playing with his cheek while contemplating larceny.

"Fifteen thousand, no questions asked," Robertson said.

Lord Edwin's fingers sped up alarmingly and he looked to his niece. Mary Anne shook her head firmly. "Fifteen thousand, eh?'' he said wistfully. ''That's a great deal of money. At Folkestone they only offered—or so Vulch tells me is the usual price—a thousand. Er, would that be pounds or guineas?''

''Guineas. No questions asked.''

Lord Edwin directed a beseeching gaze on his niece. The higher Robertson went, the more she was convinced he was a customs man. Again she shook her head and scowled fiercely to squelch her uncle's greed. Yet, there was no relying on him, and she spoke up to conclude the meeting quickly. ''If we hear anything about the silk, we'll let you know, Mr. Robertson.''

Mr. Robertson noticed Lord Edwin's peeps in his niece's direction and felt he would have better success if he could get her out of the room. ''Perhaps Miss Judson could get us some coffee, and we could discuss the matter further,'' he suggested.

''Mary Anne?'' Lord Edwin said hopefully.

''Certainly, I'll be happy to ring for Plummer.'' She went to the bell pull and yanked the rope.

To avoid the subject of selling the silk, she said, ''Mr. Robertson was attacked by Vulch's men in the stable, Uncle.''

''Yes, my dear, you already told me that. But they didn't go near the—''

''No,'' she said hastily. ''They didn't come near the house.''

But the uncle had said ''go,'' not ''come,'' Mr. Robertson noted. Now where the devil had they hidden the silk? Mary Anne saw his puzzled frown and interpreted correctly what was in his mind. ''You won't want to stay away from Vulch's too long. They'll wonder what happened to you if they happen to go to your room.''

''I particularly told them I was retiring and didn't wish

to be disturbed unless Vulch recovered the silk. I don't believe they'll be calling on me.''

Mrs. Plummer's capped head appeared at the door. "What is it then, milord?'' she asked crossly.

"Coffee, Plummer.''

"Oh, Uncle,'' Mary Anne said. "It's late, and Mrs. Plummer was in bed. Just wine, Mrs. Plummer.''

"There's wine on his desk,'' Mrs. Plummer said, pointing to the carafe.

"Why, so there is.'' Lord Edwin smiled, and poured himself a glass.

The housekeeper grumbled herself out the door, and Mary Anne poured another glass for their unwelcome guest. She sat down to show him she meant to remain. Mr. Robertson sighed and reviewed his tactics.

"This head is really aching like the devil,'' he said. "Would it put you out very much if I remained overnight, Lord Edwin?''

Mary Anne glared. He meant either to continue searching after they retired, which was bad enough, or to sneak in for a private chat with Uncle, which was worse. Uncle wouldn't last a minute against this wily intruder. He'd be in chains before morning.

"Oh, you wouldn't want to stay here,'' Lord Edwin informed him. "The place is a shambles. Wet attics, moldly bedchambers. You may count yourself lucky if there's butter for your toast in the morning. A shockingly bad run place,'' he said, as though running down an inferior hotel and not his own home.

"I'm feeling a chill,'' Mr. Robertson continued.

"Then you certainly want to hurry back to Vulch's nice, dry house,'' Lord Edwin assured him. "I'd light a fire for you, but every grate in the house smokes.''

Mr. Robertson made a staggering motion and stumbled toward a chair. He really was pale. Lord Edwin shot a questioning look at his niece. "Can hardly turn him out when he's in such a state. It would be unchristian. That is—I didn't mean to say *Christian*!" he whispered in a loud aside, and with a guilty start at the word that had cropped out.

She took her decision. Robertson was incorrigible. If he left, he'd go no farther than the stable and then soon to the barn. She could at least keep an eye on him if he was in the house, but she couldn't let him get at Uncle.

"Very well, if you're able to follow me, Mr. Robertson, I'll show you upstairs," she said stiffly, and waited till he recovered his feet before leading him off, with a warning look over her shoulder at her uncle.

As they entered the hallway, Fitch came rushing in. "I managed to—" He stopped dead in his tracks when he saw Mr. Robertson.

Lord Edwin went racing to his study door. "In here, Fitch!" he called, and pulled the lumbering giant into his office, closing the door behind him.

Mr. Robertson turned a sapient eye on his hostess. "Does that ease your alarm, Miss Judson? Fitch managed to secure the cargo."

"That's not what he meant!"

"You said earlier he was out looking for the silk."

"That was only an assumption. He was probably locking up the stable."

"After the smugglers had escaped, *sans la soie*. Yes, I speak French, also Latin and Greek, which does not make me either a French spy, a Roman gladiator, or a customs man. Is it my occasional habit of dropping a French phrase that worries you? You may hear even so unexceptionable a Royalist as Prinney spout bongjaw, I promise you."

"Does the Prince of Wales often drop into your shop?"

"*Jamais*. It is the custom for us drapers to take our samples to Carlton House."

Mary Anne took up a candelabrum from the hall table and went silently upstairs, her mind wildly scanning her options. It was easy to say you weren't a French spy or a customs man; that didn't make it so. If he wasn't a customs officer, who was he? She walked along the corridor, peering in to see if, by some miracle, Mrs. Plummer had made up any of the chambers. She hadn't. Striped ticking showed on some of the beds; others had bedspreads pulled over them, but she knew there was no linen beneath them.

"I'll have to make up a chamber for you," she said. To ensure his not returning below, she added, "Perhaps you could help. I dislike to disturb poor Mrs. Plummer again."

"By all means, let us dispense with Plummer. I don't want a piece carved out of my hide with her bread knife."

Mary Anne went to the linen closet and brought out well-worn linens. With the ease of long practice she shook out the sheets and began tucking in the ends, while Mr. Robertson struggled less expertly with his side. By this time he was virtually certain the cargo was at Horton Hall. His only aim was to secure it. If the old boy was a thief, that was nothing to him. But how could he convince the girl of this? He shouldn't have spoken so roughly earlier. He had scared the wits out of her. He must jolly her back into a trusting mood, by hinting at the truth if necessary.

He looked across the bed where she was working briskly, firming the fit of the sheet. "You do this well, Mary Anne." He smiled.

She looked up, startled at his friendly tone. "I always give Mrs. Plummer a hand around the place," she admitted.

"Bess tells me you're proficient with the beeswax and turpentine as well. A lady of many accomplishments."

"Not the customary ones. I don't paint or play the piano or embroider."

"For which I'm sure your future husband will be eternally grateful. You also don't lie very well," he said, and dropped the sheet. He sat on the edge of the bed, bringing her work to a halt.

Mary Anne took up a pillow and began to stuff it into a pillowcase. "Don't be afraid of me," he said gently. "I don't mean you or your uncle any harm. It is imperative that I get that cargo of silk. Every moment's delay could be costing lives."

She dropped the pillow and stared at him. *"Lives?"*

"Lives," he repeated firmly. "You were right in thinking there was more involved here than just silk. There is . . . something else in the cargo. Something I must find."

She stared across the bed, mesmerized. The unwanted intruder suddenly looked not at all like a customs man. His hateful tenacity took on the coloring of manly determination. "Mr. Robertson," she asked, eyes wide, "are you a—a British spy?"

He made a modest gesture of agreement. "What is it you're looking for? What was in the cargo?" she asked eagerly.

"There should have been a message from France. We have a woman planted there—she acts as a seamstress for the wives of highly placed French officials and army officers. She is frequently in their homes, where she overhears all manner of useful information. Her help has been invaluable in the past. She has dealings with the silk merchants and smuggles her findings out in cargoes of silk destined for England. It is a great secret, as I'm sure you realize. I don't want a word of this breathed abroad."

"Oh, my!" Mary Anne exclaimed, and sank onto the edge of the bed. She looked shyly at the guest and discerned the innocent air of truth in his noble aspect. His gaze was steady, his manner not at all conniving. How had she been so blind? Of course Mr. Robertson was no drapery merchant. He was obviously top of the trees, and a hero to boot. The message must be very urgent to have sent him galloping off to Dymchurch to intercept it.

"Well?" he urged.

She wet her lips and hastily reviewed her situation. Admitting to such a hero that her uncle was a thief and she an accessory proved impossible. She wanted to do it, but the words stuck in her throat. "I'll speak to Uncle and see if he knows anything. You stay here!" she ordered, and fled downstairs.

Her uncle and Fitch were in the study when she went flying in to relate her tale. When she had finished her breathless story, they both looked at her as though she were mad.

"You don't actually believe such a tale?" Uncle Edwin scoffed.

"I'm sure he's telling the truth, Uncle."

"Even if he is," Fitch pointed out, "we still can't admit to stealing. We'll have to arrange to hand the stuff over stealthily."

Mary Anne was willing to listen to any plan that would conceal her uncle's guilt.

"Christian's hut?" Lord Edwin suggested. "If you take it tonight, Fitch, the goods can be in his hands by morning. I haven't posted the letter to Codey, so he shan't be there. And if Robertson takes possession early in the morning, say at dawn, why it's himself that Codey would catch if he happened by and not us."

"He said every moment is important," Mary Anne mentioned. "Couldn't Fitch just 'find' the silk now, immediately? It could save lives, Uncle."

"Aye, and it could cost lives—ours—if he's lying," Fitch added. "He's not stupid enough to believe I just happened to find the silk as soon as we thought it safe to sell."

"You have a point," Lord Edwin agreed. "Robertson

101

isn't going to go galloping off to London to save lives in the middle of the night, and raining to boot. Fitch will move the stuff to Christian's hut tonight, and we'll tell Robertson early in the morning."

After a little arguing Mary Anne agreed to this compromise. "What shall we tell Robertson tonight?" she asked. "He's waiting upstairs. I told him I'd speak to you."

Her uncle scowled at her. "Why didn't you just tell him I was guilty? Tell him I'm exerting every effort and expect to have found the stuff by morning." This sounded unconvincing, even to his undemanding self. "Tell him Fitch is on to something," he added, and smiled.

"All right." Mary Anne went so quickly to the door that Mr. Robertson hadn't time to scamper upstairs without being seen. He had overheard every word through the keyhole, but what he had not learned was where they had the stuff hidden. This was no real problem, however. All he had to do was follow the amiable giant when he went to move it. He'd have his message tonight, instead of waiting for morning. He slipped quietly out the front door and skulked in the shadows, waiting for Fitch to come out.

Mary Anne rehearsed what she would say, and when she went to his door, she had her story ready. She tapped lightly and waited. She knocked harder and waited again. Perhaps Mr. Robertson had been undressing. After a third knock her suspicions allowed her to open the door wide, even if it meant seeing Mr. Robertson in his linen. She cast one brief look around the empty room before darting downstairs to Uncle's study.

"He's gone!" she exclaimed.

Fitch was still there, receiving last-minute instructions. The three exchanged startled glances that soon deepened to distrust and fear.

"The silk!" Fitch exclaimed, and they all three ran for the door.

Chapter Ten

Mary Anne reached the door first. Anxiety muddled her thinking, but through the mists of confusion, she suddenly got hold of one vital fact. She removed her hand from the doorknob and said, "Wait!"

"What is it?" her uncle demanded.

"We better not go out there. If Robertson is gone—"

"He *is* gone," Fitch said. "And we have a pretty good notion where he's gone to. We've got to stop him."

"He has no way of knowing where you hid the stuff," she pointed out. "He's probably lurking outside to follow us. Let us wait a moment and think what should be done."

But she found scheming beyond her. What was in her mind was the question: Is he really a British spy, or is he something else? Why had he left the room, when she told him she would cooperate?

"He's trying to get my silk without paying me!" Lord Edwin said angrily. The man must be stopped, but searching for him in the rain, hitting him, quite possibly being hit back . . . Robertson wasn't the sort to cave in without a fight—all that unpleasantness was no job for a gentleman. "Take care of him, Fitch. You may use your fists if necessary."

"Necessary, hah!" Fitch grinned from ear to ear and

began prancing around with his fists raised, ready for action.

"But if he is really working for the government—" Mary Anne objected.

"Pooh! He's working for himself and Vulch," her uncle riposted. They all retired to the study for further arguing.

In the shadows beyond, Mr. Robertson became impatient with waiting. What the devil was keeping the amiable giant? He regretted that he hadn't gotten back to his room in time for Mary Anne's visit. Naturally he had to follow her and confirm it wasn't another stunt. He didn't want to wait till morning to recover his message, either. But they were willing to help. He might have coerced her into leading him to the stuff tonight. It was beginning to look as if Fitch wasn't going to move it. His having run off made them change their minds. What was the best course? He cudgeled his brains and was struck with an idea. His mount—he didn't want it left out all night. It was a passable excuse.

Within five minutes Mr. Robertson entered the front door, making no effort at secrecy. In fact, he stamped his feet and made as much racket as he could. It was enough to bring his quarry into the hall.

"Good evening—again." He smiled easily and shook the raindrops from his head. "I just remembered I had left my nag tethered to a tree in the park. I put him in your stable—I hope you don't mind, Lord Edwin?"

The three exchanged a questioning look. "Sorry I disturbed you," Mr. Robertson said, after a small bow, he walked nonchalantly upstairs.

He missed Mary Anne's smile of relief, which would have given him pleasure on more than one score. "So that's where he was!" she said.

"Do you believe him?" Fitch asked.

"Of course! He wasn't trying to slip in quietly. Why,

he made a dreadful racket. It was all perfectly innocent. We shall proceed with the original plan. You go out and start moving the stuff, Fitch, and Uncle and I will keep an eye to see Mr. Robertson doesn't escape.''

''We'll lock his bedroom door,'' Uncle Edwin said.

''Oh, Uncle! You can't do that! It would look so very odd—as if he were our prisoner. Besides, he'll only climb out the window.''

''That he'll not,'' Fitch objected. ''Them windows haven't budged in a decade. They're as good as nailed shut, the wood's so swollen with rain getting in.''

''I'll lock his door,'' Lord Edwin repeated. ''I shan't get a wink's sleep if I don't. I'll do it cagily—drop in and offer him a nightcap, and when I leave, I'll rattle the knob a moment to cover the sound while I turn the lock.''

Mary Anne still disliked to consider what Mr. Robertson would think of their hospitality if he tried to leave his room for any innocent reason and found he was incarcerated. ''It would help if you could get him bosky,'' she suggested. ''I told him I'd speak to you, so he won't be surprised at the visit.''

''Excellent!'' Lord Edwin exclaimed. ''I'll take up a bottle of my best port. Two bottles.''

''Why not put a little laudanum in one?'' Fitch said with a crafty look. ''Plummer has a bottle in the kitchen.''

''Not too much!'' Mary Anne warned. ''We want him awake at dawn.''

''I know just what quantity gives you a good night's sleep. Five drops,'' Lord Edwin said. ''That's what Plummer gave me when that cursed molar of mine acted up last year.''

This plan satisfied them all. ''If we're sure Mr. Robertson is asleep, you and I can help Fitch, Uncle,'' Mary Anne suggested.

Lord Edwin looked at her as though she were mad. Help Fitch—in this downpour! With his sore joints?

Mary Anne stationed herself a few yards down the hall to keep a discreet guard on Mr. Robertson's door while Lord Edwin got the wine and laudanum and Fitch went to begin moving the silk to Christian's hut. When Lord Edwin had the corks removed and one bottle doctored with laudanum, he winked at Mary Anne and she scuttled along to her bedroom.

Her fears and doubts had ebbed to manageable excitement. She lay on the bed thinking, waiting till Mr. Robertson would have had time to fall asleep. She was sorry he'd be dashing off to London tomorrow as soon as he found the secret message in the cargo of silk, but she felt certain she'd see him again. Apparently he worked regularly with Vulch. If he got away early enough tomorrow morning, he might even return for the spring assembly that night. She would wear her new shawl, and they'd waltz . . .

Mr. Robertson was on fidgets waiting for the visit. He was in little doubt as to why Lord Edwin came with two bottles of wine. Did the old fool really think one bottle would put him to sleep? No, of course not. He would have laced one bottle with a sleeping draught. Yes, sure enough, the two bottles were open already, and he kept looking at them. Not clever of Lord Eddie to have put the doctored bottle in his left hand. To confirm the stunt, Mr. Robertson reached for the bottle in his right hand and swallowed his smile to see Lord Edwin awkwardly shove his left hand forward.

"This one's for you, Mr. Robertson."

"Thank you. This is a delightful surprise. I could use a drink to put me to sleep."

"Eh?" Lord Edwin gasped with a guilty start. "Sleep, you say? Why, where did you get that idea?"

"Wine always make me drowsy." Mr. Robertson smiled blandly and lifted the bottle to his lips. It was easier to hide the fact that he wasn't actually drinking anything if he kept the colored bottle. A glass would reveal the truth. He tasted the bitter trace of laudanum beneath the grape. It wasn't strong—he wouldn't have noticed it had he not been looking for it.

They sat down, and conversation turned to the important subject of silk. "Your niece spoke to you?" Mr. Robertson asked.

"She did. As it happens, Fitch had just got a line on something." Lord Edwin nodded importantly.

"That's excellent news. Your Fitch seems a bright lad."

"Fitch bright? Why, he's dull as those muddy windowpanes," Lord Edwin asserted. "Strong, but not bright. He did happen to get a line on the silk, however."

"When do you think I might get it?" Mr. Robertson asked.

"At dawn tomorrow."

"I hope the demmed rain has let up by then," Mr. Robertson remarked, and strolled to the widow as though checking the weather.

This raised no panic in his host's breast. He'd see nothing from that window. Fitch would take the shortest route, which was by the opposite side of the house. He rose and joined Robertson at the window. Both left their bottles behind.

"Did you see something move out there?" Mr. Robertson asked, and pressed his nose against the pane. He already knew the window didn't open. He had tested that as soon as he was alone in the room.

"Eh? Impossible? He wouldn't come this way." Lord Edwin pressed his nose against the pane, too. Mr. Robertson edged back to give him a clear view.

"There, didn't you see that?" he asked.

107

While Lord Edwin peered into the impenetrable blackness beyond, Mr. Robertson quickly moved to the table and switched the bottles of wine about.

"I don't see a thing," Lord Edwin said, worried now. "You don't think it was Codey?"

"Perhaps it was just a shadow," Mr. Robertson allowed, and resumed his seat.

Lord Edwin did likewise and soon picked up the doctored bottle of wine. "That's what it was, a shadow. Codey would be in his nook at the tavern by this time. A shocking bad revenue officer. I shouldn't be surprised if he's in Vulch's pocket. I mean it stands to reason; the whole parish knows Vulch lands the goods at his very dock. How does it come Codey never catches him, eh?"

Mr. Robertson took a long drink from the bottle. Lord Edwin smiled like a lady who has just received an offer from her suitor and said, "Not that I give a tinker's curse. I like my brandy as well as the next fellow."

"I'll arrange to get you a barrel as a bonus when I recover the silk."

"Demmed decent of you, Mr. Robertson."

The conversation became more congenial as the bottles emptied. Lord Edwin began yawning into his fist, and to keep suspicion at bay, Mr. Robertson did likewise. "Do you mind if I lie down, Lord Edwin?" he asked when the wine was nearly gone. He walked on unsteady legs toward the bed.

"Good idea. I'll join you," his host said. Lord Edwin fell in a heap on the floor as soon as he got off his chair.

Mr. Robertson lifted him onto the bed and hastily rifled his pockets. He recognized a bedroom key when he saw one, and before Lord Edwin had emitted the first of a series of stertorous snorts, he was locked in the room, dead to the world. Mr. Robertson took a look up and down the empty hallway before slipping quietly down the staircase and out the front door.

At eleven o'clock approximately an hour had elapsed, and Mary Anne figured it was safe to go and talk to Uncle. It had occurred to her that while Codey wasn't likely to venture out in such raw weather, Vulch's smugglers were made of hardier stuff. They'd already been there once tonight. If they returned and caught Fitch moving the silk . . . A tremble of fear shook her. She changed into her oldest slippers and went quietly down the hall. As she passed Robertson's door, she quietly tried the knob. The door was securely locked. When she saw Lord Edwin's room empty, she went in search of him downstairs. The office, too, was dark and vacant.

She had misjudged her uncle. Some latent trace of gallantry had urged him to let her rest while he went to Fitch's assistance. He could still surprise her upon occasion. Her birthday, for instance. That lovely shawl, and dinner at the inn. She went out by the kitchen, pulling her oldest shawl over her head and shoulders as she went.

The rain had ebbed to a drizzly mist. No actual drops fell, but the air was so laden with moisture that it felt clammy and surprisingly warm. Phantom clouds of fog clung to the ground, enshrouding her to the knees. She stood listening, but the only sound in the darkness was the occasional plop of water falling from leaves and roof to the ground. One particularly large drop struck her head, and she moved away from the roof into the night.

She could scarcely see beyond her nose and was cheered to know that Vulch's men would be similarly hampered. They lacked her advantage of knowing where to look for Fitch and the silk. She struck off first toward Christian's hut. Fitch should have had time to deliver one load and be on his way back. She checked for intruders, peering into shadows as she went, listening for the whicker of a horse, the rattle of a harness, or human sounds. All was silent. Her feet made no sound as they flew over the familiar terrain, skirting instinctively around the invisible thorn bush at the edge of the meadow, veering left around the sudden apparition of white, which was a wild apple tree in blossom.

At the edge of the meadow that abutted Christian's property, she stopped. She thought she could hear if Fitch were coming toward her, and in any case, she had no intention of striking into the spinney alone at night. She turned back toward the barn, hurrying over the rough ground. When she was about six yards from the building, she heard Fitch's voice. Uncle was there, then, she thought, and picked up the pace.

"A *goat*! You let a bloody goat *eat* it!" a voice shouted, with no effort at concealment.

Mary Anne stopped dead in her tracks. It wasn't Uncle's wavering tone or the coarse voice of Fitch that assailed her ears. It was the unmistakable accents of Mr. Robertson! His words made little impression on her. It was his presence on the scene that filled her with dread. How had he gotten here? Hadn't he drunk the doctored wine? He should be sound asleep by now.

"Damme, how did I know Belle would eat the stuff?" Fitch shouted back.

She listened, drawing closer behind the concealment of the barn, and peeked through a space between loose boards. Fitch had lit a rush light to let him see what he was about. She should have warned him not to! Its dim illumination seemed as bright as a beacon. In the circle of light it provided she saw two bales of silk had been opened. One sat in the mud—a lovely gold silk. It bore traces of Belle's teeth in its frayed and gnawed edges. The other bale was green. It was undamaged, as far as she could see. Belle had strayed off to a corner, foraging for new fodder.

"By God, you'll hang from the gibbet for this!" Mr. Robertson growled, and stepped forward to grab Fitch's arm.

Staring into the barn, Mary Anne felt a shot of alarm. Fitch would kill him! Then it occurred to her that Mr. Robertson carried a pistol, and she looked harder for evidence that he meant to use it.

Fitch shoved him off. He wouldn't have done that if Mr. Robertson had drawn his pistol. "How the bloody hell were we supposed to know?" Fitch demanded.

"You weren't! If you weren't a parcel of thieving scoundrels, this wouldn't have happened."

She still didn't see any pistol, but the two men were squaring off for a fistfight. Poor Mr. Robertson! She stood ready to call Fitch off if he became too rough. While she stood biting her knuckle to keep from crying out, Mr. Robertson's fist flashed out and caught Fitch on the corner of the jaw. He fell back, but it would take more than a fist to fell that giant. Mr. Robertson's fist rose again, this time catching Fitch in the stomach. There was a pained grunt; then Fitch straightened up and leveled a murderous scowl at his opponent.

As he danced around Robertson, fists raised and pawing the air, he said, "I ought to warn you, lad, I'm no amateur with my dabs. I've flattened many an opponent, and it'll be a pleasure to do the same to you."

On this menacing speech he lifted a clenched fist the size of a ham hock, and an ugly thud rent the air. Mr. Robertson dodged and caught the blow on the corner of his chin, which was all that saved him from collapse. Even the grazing blow left his head singing. He shook his head and sized up his opponent. He knew he was outweighed by seven or eight stone. Fitch was ungainly and slow on

111

his feet, like most large men, but he had some science. So had Mr. Robertson, but he felt instinctively that the less gentlemanly brawling tactics learned in back alleys would be more effective here. He joined his two hands together and threw them with all his strength in the pit of Fitch's stomach. The giant stumbled, and Mr. Robertson rushed in with a shower of blows. It was like hitting a wall. The man was solid muscle.

Fitch didn't fall, but he kept being pushed back into the barn, like a man retreating from the onslaught of a midge or an unwelcome bee. Belle came running forward to see the excitement and butted against the back of his knees. Seeing this unexpected advantage, Robertson gave a hard shove, and Fitch fell over the goat. There was a loud thump as his head struck a beam. Robertson kicked the goat aside and went to check the damage.

His satisfied snort told Mary Anne that Fitch was momentarily stunned. She stood uncertainly while Robertson looked around for something to tie Fitch up with. Yes, that's what he was doing. He ran after Belle and began untying the rope from her neck. There never was any point tying Belle up. Ropes were one of her favorite treats.

"You'll hang from the gibbet," he had said. And so would Uncle. She couldn't let him get away. She looked all around, trying to think of a weapon. At the edge of the circle of light in the barn was a piece of wood, of the sort Fitch chopped for the kitchen grate. The effectual Mr. Robertson had already got the rope from Belle's neck and was going to tie Fitch up. This was her chance, while he was bent over, his attention distracted. She whirled around the corner of the barn, snatched up the piece of wood, and inched silently forward. Instinct fought against her. She didn't want to hurt Mr. Robertson, but she couldn't let him hang Fitch and Uncle—and possibly herself. She lifted the piece of wood and brought it down on his head. The blow sounded dreadfully loud. Oh, God, had she killed him?

Fitch grunted to life and sat up. "Hey, what are you doing here, missie?" he demanded. In this moment of stress, all formality of servant and mistress was abandoned.

"Tie him up quickly, Fitch, before he wakes up," she said, and grabbed the rope from Robertson's hands.

"Aye, I will, then, till we have time to consult Lord Eddie. Best go and get him, missie."

"See if he has a gun, Fitch."

Fitch rifled Robertson's pockets and drew out the pistol. He smiled at it. "He fights fair, I'll say that for 'un," he said, and stuck the pistol in his waistband. "You'd best get along," he said to Mary Anne.

"Yes," she said, and ran off to the house, glad to put distance between herself and her crime.

She went first to her uncle's study, since he hadn't been in his room earlier. Nothing. Next she pelted up to his bedchamber, hoping he was there, since he wasn't with Fitch and he wasn't in his study. His room was still vacant. She tried to think, but what whirled in her brain was the awful image of Mr. Robertson and the echo of that hollow thump as she had hit him. Why had she done such a horrid thing? Yet, what else could she do?

She rushed into the hallway and went to Mr. Robertson's door. It was locked. Fitch said the window didn't open. How had he gotten out? The man was a magician. Popping out of locked rooms and making Uncle disappear. In desperation she pulled a key from the door across the hall and opened Robertson's room, because she didn't know where else to look. And there on the bed, the flickering flame of a single candle playing over his inert face, making him look dreadfully like a corpse, was Uncle Edwin.

Her first awful thought was that Robertson had killed him, till she spotted the empty wine bottles. Only asleep, then. Robertson had discovered their trick and played one of his own. Who could she turn to for help? Mrs. Plummer was worse than useless. She had already proclaimed herself deaf and blind in the matter. Vulch occurred to her, only to be rejected. He was Robertson's colleague. Joseph? Her flesh crawled to think what hold that would give him over Uncle and herself.

She would consult with Fitch. Maybe he could think of someone. She ran back downstairs, out the front door, pell-mell into the black night. Her terror mounted as she ran. She imagined someone was following her. Wasn't that a footfall? She looked over her shoulder. Surely something moved, there in the black night. She picked up the pace and told herself it was only nerves. No one was following her.

She could think of no possible extrication from this coil but for Uncle, Fitch, and herself to run far away and never come back. And Uncle wasn't even awake. They'd have to carry him down to the carriage. How far could they get before Robertson, the magician, freed himself and came after them?

How had they got into such a dreadful scrape? It was all Uncle's larcenous stealing of the cargo. For a thousand pounds he had ruined the reputation of the family and put all their lives in jeopardy. A tear scalded her eye as she ran. She wouldn't be going to the spring assembly. The highlight of the social year snatched from her. And she wouldn't be waltzing with Mr. Robertson in her new shawl. He'd be standing up with Bess Vulch. Wouldn't Bess smirk to hear this tale!

Fitch was pacing back and forth in front of the barn. "Where's Lord Eddie?" he demanded.

"Sound asleep. He must have drunk the doctored wine, Fitch. What are we to do?"

From the bowels of the barn, a bored voice cut into the night. "For starters, you can untie me!" Mr. Robertson called.

Mary Anne winced. She couldn't bear to face him, yet she couldn't stay away. She peered into the barn. Fitch, in an excess of eagerness, had trussed Mr. Robertson up like a goose for the oven. His knees were pulled against his chest, the same rope also binding his arms behind his back. He looked exceedingly uncomfortable there in the dust, with a dribble of blood oozing from the corner of his mouth and his stylish black hair falling over his forehead.

"Oh, Fitch! Must you tie him like that?" she exclaimed.

"The rope was too short to do it any other way."

"May I suggest—another rope?" Mr. Robertson called.

"We can at least tie him up more comfortably," Mary Anne said, and with a leary look at Fitch, she went uncertainly into the barn.

Chapter Eleven

Mr. Robertson looked up from his ignominious position in the dust. The shadows of night lent a murderous touch to his scowl and the dark eyes that raked her. "I shall be eternally grateful for your *help*, Miss Judson," he said ironically.

Mary Anne looked at him, the finest gentleman who had ever come to Dymchurch, and with her help, he had ended up in this situation. Frustration simmered to a boil till she could no longer contain it. "It's all your own fault! I *tried* to help you. If you had drunk the wine as you were supposed to . . ."

"Accessory to stealing wasn't enough for you? You prefer the gibbet to Bridewell, I assume. You know my position here. Whatever your henchmen's guilt, *you* are guilty of nothing less than treason!"

"Miss Judson had nothing to do with it!" Fitch announced. "As to the gibbet, they've got to catch us before they can hang us."

"Unless you plan to escalate your crimes to include murdering an officer of the Crown, I shall personally make it my aim to see you're caught," Mr. Robertson said, and smiled grimly. "There'll be a whole regiment scouring the countryside for me by morning."

His words smote her cruelly. Mary Anne felt the blood drain from her face. She turned to Fitch. "It's a message from France," he explained aside. "Belle ate it, you see."

"Ate the message from France?" He nodded. "Oh, dear," she said, and felt quite weak. "Are you sure, Fitch?"

"He said it should be in the bale marked with a *V*. That's the one Belle tore open," Fitch replied. "We've pawed through the silk a dozen times. It's gone."

They looked to the ground, where even now Belle was nibbling at the cargo. It was an oilskin wrapping that engaged her interest at this point. She had the corner of it in her mouth and was wagging her head in an effort to detach a piece.

"If you'd put the silk in the loft as Uncle wanted, this wouldn't have happened," Mary Anne scolded, and immediately regretted it. "I'm sorry, Fitch. It's not your fault. Are you sure the message isn't in one of the other bales?"

"We opened a couple more. It ain't here. It's always in the bale marked with a *V*, he says. Old Belle ate herself free while I was loading up and got at the bale. Pity."

The gig was half-loaded. "Let's open the rest of it, just to be sure," she said.

"I suggest you use your time more fruitfully and untie me," Mr. Robertson said imperiously. "The message is not in any of the other bales. They all come directly from the merchants. Mrs. Lalonde marks hers with a *V* and sends it along separately via one of the smugglers, who adds it to the lot."

Mary Anne looked at him uncertainly. She was sure his legs and arms must be sound asleep by this time, but she was afraid if they untied him, he'd overpower Fitch and escape.

"It's your own fault!" she charged again, because she could think of nothing sensible to say.

"Sorry I couldn't oblige you in the matter of the laudanum, but I had duties to perform. Every moment you delay me adds to your guilt. It is crucial that I get to London at once and report this."

Mary Anne turned her back to him for some private talk with Fitch. "Perhaps we should just let him go," she said doubtfully.

"Lord Eddie'd have my head on a platter if I did. I'll go and see if I can rouse him up. You'll be safe here. I tied the customer up right and tight."

"Couldn't you at least loosen his feet? He looks so terribly uncomfortable."

"Maybe it'll teach him some manners. At least it won't kill him for ten minutes." Fitch laughed and lumbered off into the night, leaving Mary Anne behind to guard the troublesome prisoner.

They eyed each other warily. "What was in the message?" she asked. Mr. Robertson began surreptitiously moving his wrists back and forth behind his back, trying to loosen the bindings.

"If I knew that, I wouldn't be so distraught at its loss. It contained whatever military matters Mrs. Lalonde was able to discover for us. Perhaps the imminent invasion of England by Boney," he added to frighten her. "If the country falls into his clutches due to your efforts . . ."

"I'm not the one who stole the silk! I didn't know a thing about it till tonight."

"What were you doing, going to visit the Frenchies in the meadow yesterday morning?" He stirred restively, as though to get comfortable, while he continued wrenching his wrists back and forth. The friction of the rough rope scraped the skin from his wrists, but the rope was loosening a little.

118

"I wasn't visiting them!"

"Were you not? You were all but embracing the ring-leader when I so inconveniently interrupted you. Were you reporting your success in intercepting the message, Miss Judson? Are you working for the enemy?"

She stared, unable to conceive he really believed such a thing. Nor did he, but he wished to show her the extent of the case that could be made against her if she didn't cooperate and free him. Fitch had bound him so tightly, it seemed impossible to work loose. He felt instinctively she was the likeliest one to give in.

"Certainly not! You saw for yourself that I cried for help! I had no idea they were there."

"I rather think that cry for help came after you spotted me, however. You looked very relieved when I later told you the Frenchies had been allowed to escape."

"Of course I was relieved. No one likes to think there are Frenchmen prowling the neighborhood."

"I might be able to convince the courts you're telling the truth if you help me," he tempted.

"Uncle will decide. He'll be here in a minute."

"He won't be here before morning, and we both know it. Yes, I know it's my own fault for letting him drink my wine. I wonder what the judge will think of your trying to poison me."

"There wasn't enough laudanum in it to kill you. We just wanted time to—to . . ."

"Yes?" he encouraged. His hands were beginning to go numb from the rope, and his wrists were cut to raw flesh. "What was your plan?"

"Well, I suppose there's no harm in telling you now, since you already think the worst of us. Uncle wanted to sell the stuff to you, but he didn't want it to be done here on his property. Fitch was moving it to Christian's hut, where the Frenchies were yesterday. Fitch was going to wear a mask and arrange the sale. It was only the money Uncle wanted, not the message."

Mr. Robertson sighed at their naïveté. He would have recognized Fitch in a second. There weren't two such giants in all of Kent. He could almost feel sorry for these innocent crooks—especially Mary Anne—but this wasn't the moment to be soft. "*Only* the money. *Only* stealing," he said satirically. "Lord Edwin will add great luster to the family name when this gets out."

"He was only stealing from the Frenchies!" she pointed out. "Vulch hadn't paid for the silk. Why, it's an Englishman's duty to get what he can from the French at this time. They'd just buy cannons with the blunt."

"And Lord Edwin will buy brandy—to return the money to French coffers. That sort of rationalization cuts no ice with me. The man is a common thief at best." On this lofty speech he turned his head aside and began looking around the barn for weapons to defend himself when Fitch returned, as Fitch had taken his pistol.

The fight went out of her at the condemning phrase. It was true. Uncle was a thief, and Mr. Robertson rightfully despised him—and her. They were beneath reproach. All she could do to redeem herself in his eyes was to show him she was at least a ladylike thief.

"Would you like some water?" she asked after a moment. "There's a pump outside that's used for the cow. The water's perfectly clean."

"More to the point, I'd like you to loosen this rope. My feet at least."

"You could run away if I did."

"My hands, then."

"Then you could untie your feet." She frowned in perplexity, hoping to convey that she'd help him if she could. Surely he could see her position.

"Some compromise must be possible. Tie my feet up

120

with another rope, and at least get me out of this knot,'' he suggested.

He did look very uncomfortable. She looked around the barn for another rope. "I don't see any," she said.

"Use my cravat."

His lovely white cravat was covered with dust and a few drops that looked black but must be blood. "Well, I suppose there wouldn't be any harm in that," she said, and went forward warily to undo his cravat.

She felt self-conscious touching him. An air of intimacy built around them as his breaths fanned her cheek and her hand brushed his chin. Her fingers trembled as she fumbled with the linen.

When he spoke, his voice was low-pitched, very close to her ear. His words were mundane in the extreme, but she felt goose bumps lift the hair on her arms. "Would you mind wiping that blood from my mouth?" he asked. "It's like Chinese torture, feeling it trickle slowly."

She drew the cravat away carefully, as though it would scrape his neck, and dabbed at the congealing blood. "Your lip's split," she said. "I should really wash it."

"You could wet the cravat at the pump," he suggested, and looked up at the rush light, stuck into one of the stalls. It wasn't placed very high. Perhaps he could hobble on his knees and dislodge it while she was at the pump. If he could burn the ropes off . . .

"Yes, I'll do that," she said, and hopped up.

The trouble was, he didn't remember seeing any pump outside. If it was a few yards away, he might have time. But almost instantly he heard the squawking of a pump handle and realized she was just outside the door. She was back even before he had managed to get on his knees.

"This may hurt a little," she warned, and knelt down in the dust to daub tenderly at the cut.

From his foreshortened view of her face, he saw long

121

lashes resting fanlike on her pale cheeks. Her hair curled in wispy tendrils around her forehead from the moisture. Naturally curly hair, a pretty chestnut shade. Her forehead was pinched in consternation. Her touch was exquisitely gentle, shy. He felt a weakening stab of pity for this pretty provincial and tried to shake it away. Then she lifted her long lashes and stared at him.

"I'm sorry. Did I hurt you?" she asked softly.

He didn't answer. In fact, he hadn't heard actual words, only her dove-soft voice. His attention was all focused on her eyes, which dazzled him at this close range. "Mary Anne," he said, so softly she wasn't sure she hadn't imagined it. His voice was a seductive sigh.

I believe he's going to kiss me! she thought, and instinctively pulled back an inch. It gave him a clearer view of her face, which was an enchantingly pale oval in the dim rush light. "You're very beautiful," he said softly.

A smile trembled on her lips. "Do you really think so, Mr. Robertson?" she asked.

"From the moment I saw you at the inn."

She gazed unblinkingly into his eyes. "I thought you were very handsome," she said. Then, afraid that she was being forward, she added, "Bess thought so, too."

Mr. Robertson's lips curved into a smile at this peculiar addition. He wasn't accustomed to having a third party drawn into his lovemaking. "Bess doesn't treat me so shamelessly," he said leadingly.

"You don't have to tell me! She'd treat you even better if you weren't a—that is . . ."

"A drapery merchant?"

"I don't think there's anything wrong with it!" she assured him.

"I'm more than a drapery merchant, Mary Anne. You know why I'm here. Help me. You must let me go before Fitch returns."

Her face froze in anger. "Don't think to con me with sweet talk, sir! You didn't mean a word of it, did you? You were only trying to charm me into setting you free so you could turn us all in. You must think I'm a regular greenhorn." She hopped up and turned away to hide the tears that gathered in her eyes.

She felt like an idiot, but at least she hadn't loosened his bindings, and she wouldn't. He could grow into a humpback for all she cared. She strode angrily from the barn to wait for Fitch and left Mr. Robertson, still tied in knots and alone, to regret his poor timing.

He also regretted the loss of the message from France, but as the thing was done, there was no point repining. All he could do now was send word to Whitehall and await the next message. Dymchurch was as good a place to wait as London. And it would be amusing to roast his captors. He thought of all this as he worked to free his wrists.

Mary Anne had plenty of time to think, too, for Fitch didn't come back for another ten minutes. Of course she knew that she and Uncle and Fitch were now outlaws, condemned to a life of running. If caught, they were for the gibbet, but this received less than a minute of her time. Mostly she thought of that moment when Mr. Robertson had gazed into her eyes and said, "You're very beautiful." He had looked as though he wanted to kiss her. What would it have been like?

At length Fitch returned. "I can't rouse the old gaffer," he said. "He's dead to the world. We'll just have to leave Robertson trussed up till morning."

Much as she disliked to agree, Mary Anne could find no other way out of their problem. "At least tie his arms and legs separately. We don't want to cripple the poor man. But make sure you don't let him get away from you. I'll go back to the Hall and send Uncle down the minute he wakes up. And, Fitch—you could put that old horse blanket over Mr. Robertson. It'll be chilly before morning."

"I'll do what needs doing, never fear. You get along home, missie."

Mary Anne scampered back to the Hall. She felt a hundred years old as she climbed the long staircase to her room. She looked in at Uncle and tried to rouse him, but he only smiled softly in his sleep, dreaming who knew what impossible thing. Perhaps that he had sold the silk and had his ill-gotten gains. She went wearily to her room and slept on top of the bed in her gown because she was too desolate to bother changing.

Chapter Twelve

As the first red glow of dawn lightened the horizon, Mary Anne stirred and sat up. What day was it? Saturday—the assembly! She sat in confusion a moment, wondering why she was dressed. Then she remembered the whole dreadful situation and sighed. She'd best get ready for the ordeals of the day. She washed up and put on her second-best sprigged muslin before going to the room where her uncle had spent the night.

Lord Edwin was still asleep, but the stertorous snores had dwindled to a rumble, and after she gave him a few shakes, he opened his close-set eyes and said, "Yes, yes, I'm awake. Oh, my head! It feels like a sack of rocks."

His eyes were as red as a ferret's, made to look even worse in his ashen face. "That was a bad bottle of wine I drank last night," he said, shaking his head. "Well, what is it, Mary Anne. Is Fitch ready to arrange the deal with Robertson?"

She explained the true situation to him two or three times till he grasped all the awful ramifications. He seemed to shrivel before her very eyes. Was this shrunken, frightened, foolish old man to be her savior? She knew in her bones Uncle had no more idea how to rescue them than she had herself.

"But this is dreadful!" he worried, wringing his hands. "I should have known better than to trust Fitch. Why didn't he make a clean job of it and finish the bleater? And he let Belle eat the message, eh? Serves Robertson right, hiding a message in a bale of silk. Whoever heard of such a way of carrying on? He should have known Belle would eat it. She eats everything. Why couldn't she have used her goat brain and eaten Robertson? Well, don't look to me missie. I don't know how you are to extricate yourself. Tell Plummer to make a gallon of coffee. I'll be down immediately."

It occurred to Mary Anne that their prisoner must also have coffee and something to eat. "I'll need a breakfast tray, Mrs. Plummer," she said when she had given the order for coffee.

"Lord Edwin invited Robertson to stay overnight, did he?" Mrs. Plummer asked.

"Yes—that is, not invited, exactly. He's tied up, a prisoner in the barn."

Mrs. Plummer threw up her hands in horror. "Don't tell me anything! I didn't hear you. I'll prepare a tray for you to take upstairs to Mr. Robertson. I'll not swing in the wind for your uncle's sins, and if you was wise, missie, you'd keep away from it, too."

"I wish I had kept away from it," Mary Anne said, but she helped with Mr. Robertson's breakfast, choosing the choice cuts of ham for him and adding a pot of marmalade to go with his toast.

"You'll all end up in Newgate," Mrs. Plummer repined as she worked. "Holding an officer of the Crown prisoner—why, you might as well take a knife and put it through the prince hisself. And Vulch will be here looking for him before the sun gets much higher. You can't leave him sitting in the barn for any passerby to see."

"I know," Mary Anne said. "We'll have to put him in the cellar or attic."

"Let me know when you're bringing him, and I'll leave the house. I don't want to know nothing about it. I suggest the cellar. If you're going to have to feed him, you don't want to be climbing all them stairs up to the rafters."

These alternatives were discussed as Miss Judson and Lord Edwin wended their way toward the barn. It promised to be a beautiful day. The newly washed greenery glowed in the early sunlight, and birds chirped overhead, all ignored by the troubled pair. Mary Anne carried the best silver tray, covered with a white tea towel to protect the food, and Lord Edwin acted as lookout, to see they weren't spotted.

At the barn door he stopped. "It isn't necessary for me to go in," he said. "I mean to say, whatever the fellow wants, he can tell you, Mary Anne. I daresay you could turn him up sweet better than an old reprobate like myself. Be nice to him. This may all blow over yet. A pretty girl and a bachelor—here's your chance to nab yourself a parti. *Dulce et decorum est*, as the Latins say," he quoted, with awful inappropriateness. "Especially *decorum*—remember you're a lady."

She stared at his nonsense. "Someone will have to feed him, Uncle! He can't feed himself, with his hands tied."

"Untie him."

"He'll escape if we do."

"Oh, guests are troublesome things. I'm sorry I ever invited him. Fitch can feed him, then, if you're shy. Just say good morning to Robertson and give Fitch the tray."

Both men were wide-awake and glaring at each other when Mary Anne entered with the tray. She was relieved to see Fitch had rearranged the bindings to put Robertson out of his misery. He was no longer hunched over, but sitting upright against a stall with his hands tied behind his back. The horse blanket designated for Robertson's comfort was around Fitch's shoulders. Both men looked the worse for the stubble of beard that shadowed their lower faces. A glower further detracted from the prisoner's suavity but added a touch of attractive danger.

"Where's Lord Eddie?" Fitch asked.

Her eyes slid to the barn door, and Fitch headed for it. "Wait, Fitch!" she called. But, of course, Fitch didn't heed her. She realized then that Fitch needed breakfast, too, and to freshen himself after spending the night in the barn.

She looked grimly to the prisoner. "I have some breakfast here," she said, and set the tray on the ground beside him.

"I'm not hungry, thank you."

"Stubbornness won't get you anywhere, Mr. Robertson. You might as well eat. You'll need your strength to try to escape."

"I escape better when I'm awake."

"There's no laudanum in it—worse luck." Now why hadn't they thought of that?

She dragged a bale of silk toward him and sat on it, with the tray on her knees. She whisked off the cover, revealing a breakfast that still looked attractive, though it was stone cold.

While Mary Anne busied herself pouring coffee and creaming it, Mr. Robertson studied her. "What's the verdict?" he asked. "Has Lord Edwin not come to his senses? You might as well let me go. It will come to that in the end, and meanwhile I expect I'm a rather troublesome guest."

"Sugar?" she asked, ignoring his taunts.

"Two."

She stirred in two spoonfuls of sugar and held the cup

to his lips. He sipped carefully and detected no foreign substance.

"About what you said last night, Mr. Robertson . . ."

"It's the only way—unless you plan to murder me."

"I don't mean about letting you go free! You can see that's impossible. You'd only report us to the law. I was referring to something else. You said you should notify Whitehall that the message went astray. If you'll dictate the note, I'll write it up and post it for you."

"They wouldn't accept it as genuine if it weren't written in my own hand," he parried.

She lifted the cup to his lips again, and when she offered the toast, he bit off a piece. "You could send something— your ring or something else—to let them know it comes from you," she suggested.

"This is reality, Miss Judson, not a novel by Mrs. Radcliffe."

"You're not very helpful!"

"I don't make a habit of helping thieves," he sneered. As the letter had to be written, however, he added, "The superior I report to is Sir George FitzHugh at the Admiralty."

"I'll have Uncle write the note. He used to work at the Admiralty. He knows people there who can vouch for him."

"Let us hope his colleagues don't remember him too well," he said with a satirical glint in his dark eyes.

It went against the grain to recommend the ham after this snide remark. Mary Anne didn't recommend it, but she speared a piece with the fork and jabbed at his mouth.

She noticed Robertson's feet were tied with the cravat. "Fitch used the rope for your wrists, did he?" she asked.

"Yes, they're chafing rather badly. He has some hopes I'll take an infection and spare you the bother of my future care."

She was appalled to hear they had added any more wounds to the officer of the Crown. "I can get some salve if they're troubling you," she offered.

Mr. Robertson hunched his shoulders indifferently. "The letter is of more importance. It should be sent off immediately. I'd like to speak to Lord Edwin."

"He won't see you."

"Why not?"

"He's ashamed, I suppose. Uncle doesn't readily accept responsibility for his wrongdoings. I'll give him the message."

Mr. Robertson gave her a frustrated look. "You already have it. You've endangered lives by stealing the cargo of silk and losing the message from France. You endanger your own lives by holding me here. This can't go on forever. Ultimately you must free me, and by prolonging the inevitable, you only make it worse for yourselves. I had hoped to be able to convince your uncle of this, but it seems he's as mindless as you and Fitch. That's my message. Try, if you can, to convince him."

She listened but knew too well the futility of trying to talk sense to her uncle. "If you don't want any more breakfast, I'll go and get the pen and paper now. You didn't try the eggs," she said.

When she looked at the tray, she saw Belle had consumed eggs and ham, and was finishing her meal by eating the napkin.

"The letter, Miss Judson!" he said.

She put Belle out into the yard, picked up the tray, and left. Fitch had gone to freshen himself at the house and to have breakfast. Her uncle was gone, pacing back and forth beyond view of the open doorway.

"Mr. Robertson would like to talk to you," she said.

"Talk to me? Whatever for? He has a lot of gall—talk

130

to me, indeed, after feeding me doctored wine. I have a good mind to turn him off.''

''Perhaps you should, Uncle. We can't keep him here forever. Let us set him free.''

''What, to report us to the constable and pack us off to the roundhouse? I know what goes on at that roundhouse. One draught of small ale a day—that's what you get. No wine, no brandy. And the food! Why, it's worse than Plummer's ragout. Fitch was put in for a week when he beat up the greengrocer. Oh, no, they don't get me in the roundhouse, thank you.''

''It won't be the roundhouse. It will be Newgate for you and Bridewell for me.''

''There you are, then. Newgate's no better than the roundhouse. We can't set him free. And while he's out of commission, Fitch must arrange to sell the silk.''

''Oh, Uncle,'' she said wearily, and went to the Hall to get the pen and paper. Fitch was just finishing breakfast when she entered by the back door.

''How's the prisoner?'' Mrs. Plummer asked Mary Anne. ''Not that I want to know a thing about him, but it seems to me the poor soul must be in misery, all tied up and not able to tend to his natural functions.''

''His wrists are chafed from the ropes. Do you have some ointment, Mrs. Plummer?''

''Ointment ain't what I meant,'' she said severely, but she went to the cupboard and got it.

''I'll tend to him now,'' Fitch said, and left.

Mrs. Plummer took the tray. ''Your little diary will be getting more than it bargained for, eh, missie?''

''Yes, indeed, but I don't seem to have time to write in it. Oh, that reminds me. A pen and paper. Mr. Robertson must write a letter.''

''I don't want to know nothing about it. The only decent stationery in the house is in your uncle's desk. I was thinking, if Belle has mussed up one bale of silk so it can't be sold, we might get new curtains for the saloon out of it. I can dust if off. There'd be plenty for a new gown for the assembly as well if we got at it right away."

"The assembly? Oh, I can't go to that this year."

"Miss the assembly and let that bold chit of a Bess Vulch have her way with all the men? Of course you'll go. Bring up the gold silk, and I'll use your blue gown for a pattern. It will just match your shawl."

Mary Anne assembled the ointment and writing materials and returned disconsolately to the barn. It was still only six-thirty, but the countryside was already stirring. Soon Vulch would learn his guest had vanished and would be out looking for him. They'd have to move Mr. Robertson and the silk.

Lord Edwin lurked outside the barn, too ashamed to face his captive. "How is it going with you and young Robertson?" he asked hopefully. "Is he making up to you at all?"

"We've got to hide him some place better than the barn, Uncle. Vulch will soon be here looking for him."

Lord Edwin was tired of his guest and was in an irritable mood. "I wish the wretched fellow would go away. That's the trouble with commoners—they don't know when they've overstayed their welcome. Let them get a foot in the door, and they become tenants for life. If he had any gumption, he should have escaped last night. Fitch is putting the silk in the loft before Belle gobbles up the rest of it. There's ten guineas blown down the wind."

"About hiding Mr. Robertson . . ."

"Do what you and Fitch think best with him."

"Plummer suggested the cellar."

"Plummer—she's the wisest of us all. She won't hear of having anything to do with him. The cellar, eh? Why not the attic? With luck, he might drown. Well, I'm oiling

132

off to the village. Vulch won't get a sniff of me when he comes. Tell Fitch not to forget to send Black's boat back. He should have done it before now. Black likes an early start for his fishing. Fitch is useless when all's said and done. The man would forget to comb his hair if I didn't remind him.''

On this condemning speech he walked away from his duties, leaving Mary Anne in confusion. She called Fitch out to discuss the situation.

"You'd better take Black's boat back. He'll be waiting for it,'' she said.

"Where's Lord Eddie?''

"He's gone into the village.''

"What for?''

"He's just run away, Fitch. That's the top and bottom of it. After getting us into this he's abandoned us. You know how he is.''

"He takes life easy,'' Fitch agreed with no rancor. "Will you be safe with Robertson?'' he asked.

"You'd best move him to the cellar before you go, in case Vulch comes.''

"What about the silk? Shouldn't I put it in the loft first?''

"Yes—no. Oh, I don't know, Fitch,'' she said, and burst into tears.

Fitch's heart wrenched to see missie so bothered, but before he could comfort her, he was faced with another problem. Jeremy Black was legging it toward the barn, with a face that looked like thunder. If Robertson realized there was someone out there, he'd call and all would be lost. Fitch ran to greet Black.

"You were supposed to have her back by dawn,'' Black charged.

"I was just about to sail her down to your place. She's in the rushes down at the shore. Sorry, Jeremy.''

"Don't bother borrowing her again if you can't get her back when you're supposed to," he grumbled, and went off to reclaim his vessel.

It was one duty, at least, removed from Fitch's broad but not infinitely broad shoulders. Undemanding as Fitch was, even he was beginning to feel ill-used. He feared, too, that if he allowed Robertson to walk up to the Hall, the man might manage to escape. Yet, to carry a writhing, angry, large man such a distance was a formidable task.

"You'll have to help me move Robertson. You hold the gun on him while I untie his feet and walk him up to the Hall."

"A gun?" Mary Anne exclaimed. "Oh, Fitch, he knows I'd never use it."

"You untie him, then, and I'll carry the gun."

How had the simple stealing of a cargo of smuggled silk turned into such a wretched piece of work as this? Yet something must be done, and until they could decide how to untie this Gordian knot, they must keep Robertson in custody.

"All right," she said, and went reluctantly into the barn, carrying the ointment and pen and paper that she might better have left at the Hall.

Mr. Robertson's accusing black eyes and satirical sneer did nothing to lighten her mood. Fitch held the cocked pistol right at Robertson's head while Mary Anne approached him. Her heart was in her mouth, lest the gun accidentally go off.

"If you so much as look sideways, you're dead," Fitch said. In his irascible mood, he sounded as though he meant it.

Mr. Robertson did risk one sideways look. He looked at Mary Anne. It was a peculiar look: part anger, part amusement, and part sympathy. That tinge of sympathy devastated her.

Chapter Thirteen

With Fitch holding the gun to Robertson's head, Mary Anne went to his feet and untied them.

"Up on your pins," Fitch ordered.

Robertson, with a look that would freeze fire, tried to gain his feet with his hands tied behind his back. When he stumbled, Mary Anne reached out and steadied him. Every fiber of her being wanted to do more than steady him. She wanted to free his bindings and apologize. She wanted to take a brush to his lovely jacket, which was all wrinkled and muddied. She wanted to pitch herself into his arms and bawl like a baby, but all she could do with Fitch there was help him up, then follow as Fitch urged him across the park.

She sensed how his proud spirit detested this final ignominy they were inflicting on him. It could be the straw that broke the camel's back. Mr. Robertson, who used to look on her with favor, had murder in his eyes. And what would be the final upshot of it? There was no way they could keep him a prisoner forever. Before a week, before the day was out, it would be they who were prisoners. The very futility of this exercise was a further aggravation.

Around the edge of the rope, Mary Anne could see that

his hands were rubbed raw. Fitch had bound them so closely, the blood was turning his hands red and swollen.

Mrs. Plummer spotted their advance from her kitchen window and fled into her room so she could truthfully say in court she hadn't seen a sign of Mr. Robertson at the Hall after he went up to his bed the night before. She remained there till the three had gone into the cellar, and hoped Fitch and Mary Anne had the wits to leave by the side door that went directly outdoors. Mary Anne knew her feelings in the matter and could be counted on to do the decent thing. She didn't want to have to report any unusual comings or goings when she was under oath.

Mrs. Plummer decided, as she looked around her kitchen when all had fallen silent beyond her bedroom door, that she could honestly say she didn't know what had happened to her candles, though she noticed they were missing from her kitchen, and she hoped they wouldn't leave the three of them burning all day in the cellar. Her supply was down to half a dozen, and they were downright obstinate in the village about giving credit.

Below stairs, the three tallow candles did very little to dispel the gloom of a damp, dusty hole. When Robertson was safely disposed on an empty hogshead and Mary Anne had the writing paper in position, Fitch deemed it safe to return to his work. He tied Robertson's feet again with the cravat.

"I'll get the silk stashed in the loft. If you have any trouble, come to the barn," he said to Mary Anne. "I'll leave you this, just in case," he added, and handed her the pistol, which she set on a high shelf as carefully as though it might go off by itself.

When he had gone, Mary Anne cast a doleful look at her prisoner and sighed. "We'd best get on with the letter," she said.

Mr. Robertson dictated a terse note, using words that

implied it was being written by Lord Edwin Horton. Mary Anne copied it verbatim, and when it was done, she remembered that her uncle was to sign it.

"You'd best give that to your uncle at once," he said. "Too much time has elapsed already."

She was too embarrassed to tell him her uncle had sheered off. Fitch would have to take it to Dymchurch when he got the silk hidden. "Yes. Before I go, I'll just put some salve on your wrists," she said, and drew out the can.

"Never mind the wrists."

"But they looked very sore," she said. "It won't take a minute."

She was glad his hands were tied behind his back. In this way, she didn't have to look at his face and he couldn't see her. She pulled the rope a little to allow the blood to flow; it was not loose enough to let him escape.

"We never meant for it to go this far, you know," she said.

"*We?* I understood *you* were only drawn into the affair last night—just before matters took a turn for the worse," he added leadingly.

"I mean, I'm sure Uncle didn't want to take you a prisoner. In fact, I know he didn't."

"Then why don't you untie me?" he suggested.

"You know I can't!" she said, on a hiccup of regret.

Mr. Robertson found his sympathy aroused by her plight. It was ludicrous that he should feel this pity for his captors, but pity was the only emotion possible for at least this one of them. Annoyed with himself, he spoke harshly.

"You will live to regret it if you don't, Miss Judson. I might be able to keep you out of this if you help me now. Lord Edwin is only your uncle—he can't mean that much to you. The man is a fool, but gentleman enough, I trust, that he wouldn't willingly drag you into this unsavory affair. You, at least, might escape unscathed. I can be a good friend. I can also be a ruthless enemy. Otherwise, you leave me no alternative but to—''

He heard a sharp intake of breath and noticed she had become still. Her fingers no longer smoothed the ointment on his wrists. He looked over his shoulder, hoping she was coming around to his way of thinking. "Mary Anne?" he said hopefully.

She was standing perfectly rigid. Her face had become stiff with outrage. "Are you seriously suggesting I should desert Uncle when he needs me the most?" she demanded. "Leave him like a rat deserting a sinking ship and save my own skin, when I owe my very life to him? What kind of a man are you?" she asked, her voice high with disbelief. "You said you could be a good friend. I'm afraid you overestimate yourself, sir. Friends don't hurt the people they love. I wouldn't have you for a friend, not if you begged me. I'd no more trust my safety to you than I'd trust it to Bonaparte himself.

"And you don't know what kind of a man my uncle is, either. A fool, you call him. He may be foolish, but he's the kindest, dearest, most generous fool I ever met. I wish the rest of the world could be his kind of fool, that—Oh, never mind. You wouldn't understand," she said abruptly. She snapped the lid on the ointment, picked up the letter, and turned to leave, while Robertson sat stunned at her outburst.

"Try me," he said.

"You've *been* tried, Mr. Robertson. A man who could even *suggest* that I save my skin by turning in my accomplices has revealed his stripe. No doubt it is the way *you* would behave. Ladies and gentlemen have a higher standard." She tossed her head and turned toward the stairs. On an afterthought, she turned back and extinguished all the candles. In her outrage she forgot the pistol, which was out of sight.

"Leave me one light at least!" he called.

"To burn off your rope? I think not, Mr. Robertson. With luck the rats may gnaw it off for you. I make sure you will soon reach an understanding with *vermin*." On this lofty speech she went upstairs, to be met by Mrs. Plummer.

"Now what's got you all in a pelter?" Mrs. Plummer demanded. "Has the lad passed out? I thought he looked a darker shade of pale when you brought him up."

"No, he's alert and kicking."

"Did that vile creature try to get his hands on you?"

"Certainly not!"

"Then what are you crying for?"

"Because—because we're all going to prison, and Mr. Robertson is horrid."

Mrs. Plummer's eyes bulged with curiosity, but with superhuman forbearance she said, "Don't tell me nothing about it. I don't want to know, but if that heathen has lifted his hand against you, I'll go down with my butcher knife and cut it off, as the good book orders a decent Christian to do."

Mary Anne looked doubtfully at the important letter for Sir George FitzHugh and went to her uncle's office. The letter must take precedence over everything else. Whitehall must be notified that the message had gone astray. With Uncle Edwin's return so indefinite, she took up the quill and added to her crimes by forging his signature. By the time she got back to the barn, Fitch had the silk hidden safely in the hayloft.

"This must be sent to London at once," she said, and handed him the letter.

"You don't think it might bring some government men down on our heads?" he asked.

139

"I don't know, Fitch, and I don't care. We can't do anything to hinder the war effort, or we'll be in even worse trouble. Post the letter, and if you see Uncle, tell him to come home immediately."

"Aye, 'twould be helpful if he'd decide how to get this cargo to Folkestone."

"Yes, it would. We'll need the money for our escape. I think the best thing to do is for all of us to get into the carriage and flee. After six hours or so, Plummer can 'discover' Mr. Robertson in the cellar and set him free."

"Nay, it'll never come to that, missie." He laughed.

But Fitch hadn't heard how Mr. Robertson had spoken in the cellar. He was implacable, with so little of decent feelings that he even suggested she turn in her own uncle— and Fitch, who was like a big brother to her. "I fear it will, Fitch."

Fitch left, and Mary Anne went reluctantly back to the house. She felt she had fallen into a deep, dark well and would never see daylight again. The waters were closing over her head. There was no way out of this. Even if Uncle sold the silk and they managed to run away, they'd soon be caught. Caught like common thieves and locked up till it was time to execute them.

Mrs. Plummer was in the kitchen making her dreaded fish tart. "Is everything quiet downstairs?" Mary Anne asked.

"Quiet as the grave. He must've fallen asleep. If anybody happens to be in the cellar, that is to say. Not that I'd know nothing about it."

The banging of the door knocker was heard faintly from the staircase. The sound was like a death knell to Mary Anne. She felt faint and wanted to run upstairs and hide. Mrs. Plummer's face was as white as her floured hands, but she tried to put a brave face on it. "Now, who's that come to pester us?" she asked, but her voice trembled.

140

"I'll answer it," Mary Anne said.

She hastily tidied her hair and straightened her gown before going upstairs. It was a relief to see it was only Mr. Vulch come to call. The man always looked worried and despondent. Today he looked more harried than usual. His face sagged with sorrow.

"Ah, good morning, Mr. Vulch." She smiled. "I'm afraid Uncle's gone into town this morning." Hospitality urged her to offer him a glass of wine or a cup of tea, but common sense told her this wasn't the time to have a caller in the house. She spoke to him at the door.

"Is Mr. Robertson here?" he asked. Worry made his voice tense.

"No, is he missing?"

"He's been missing since last night," Vulch said. "He didn't sleep in his room. I went to have a word with him before retiring, and he was gone. His mount was gone as well."

"Oh," she said faintly. It seemed Vulch hadn't gone to her uncle's stable, then, thank God. She must tell Fitch to do something with Mr. Robertson's mount—hide it or set it free. It would find its way back to the inn. "Where— where do you think he could be?" Vulch's men knew he'd been here last night, of course.

"I made sure he was here. He's got it in his noggin your uncle knows something about that missing cargo. I begin to fear something has happened to him. He'd never have gone back to London without telling me." He eyed her suspiciously.

"I shouldn't think so. But perhaps he got called back— an urgent message . . ." she said vaguely.

"No, he received no message. I hope to God nothing's happened to him. It has something to do with the silk. That's all that would take him away so suddenly."

Mr. Vulch wouldn't be that worried about a draper,

Mary Anne thought. He knows something about Mr. Robertson's other occupation. "You seem unduly perturbed, Mr. Vulch," she said.

"I am. The fact of the matter is—"

There was a clatter of hoofbeats form the road. They both looked out, both hoping it was Lord Edwin. Mary Anne was annoyed to see Joseph Horton's white mare prancing along. To keep him from the stable, she opened the door and called in a friendly way.

"Good morning, Joseph." She turned back to Vulch. "He'll be looking for Uncle as well," she said. "Shall we go and speak to him outside?"

"Why, I thought it was yourself young Horton would be calling on!" Mr. Vulch exclaimed.

She gave a worried smile and hastened him out the door. "Mr. Vulch was just telling me Mr. Robertson's disappeared," she said. "You haven't seen anything of him along the way?"

"Disappeared? Why, what do you mean?" Joseph asked, staring from one to the other.

Mr. Vulch repeated his story, and the gentlemen exchanged a curious, meaningful look. There was something going on here that she didn't understand. Whatever Mr. Vulch's claim to perturbation, Joseph had no reason to be concerned. Vulch had been about to say something when Joseph arrived.

"What is it?" she demanded. "Why are you both looking so—so nervous?"

"It is supposed to be a great secret," Vulch said in a conspiratorial way, "but as Joseph knows, and with Robertson disappearing on us, no doubt it will soon be plastered on every tree in the parish, so I might as well tell you. The fact of the matter is, Mr. Robertson is not just a draper. No, no, he's working for the government." He nodded his head knowingly and put his finger to his lips.

"This is not to be broadcast, mind. I haven't even told my own family, but he's actually here on war business."

"Why, you don't know the half of it, Mr. Vulch," Joseph said, and laughed. "That man is not Mr. Robertson. He's Lord Dicaire. A viscount, the Earl of Pelham's eldest son. Quite the white-haired lad at Whitehall. I recognized him the minute I laid eyes on him. He was pointed out to me in London when I went to see the F.H.C. off on one of their jaunts. Of course, no one else here in the county would know him. He got me aside at once and asked me not to tell anyone. The sort of work he is presently engaged in is very confidential."

So that was why Joseph had been toadying up to Robertson! She even remembered Robertson's following Joseph to the door the first night they met at the Hall. Joseph had half recognized him then, but Robertson's performance had clouded his memory. Mary Anne felt doom engulf her. Bad enough they had a spy tied up in the cellar. Now he was a noble spy. An eminent aristocrat, the white-haired boy of Whitehall. She had never fainted in her life, but she thought she was going to faint now and almost wished she could.

"A lord! You don't mean it!" Vulch exclaimed, eyes bulging. "Wait till I tell my wife this. She entertaining a lord and not knowing it. And Bess not having the wits to throw her bonnet at him. I wondered how he got that search warrant for Lord Edwin's house so quickly. He said he traveled with one because of the sort of work he does. I know all about his work," he informed Joseph. "So he is Lord Dicaire. Well, well, here are we entertaining angels unaware," Vulch said in an excess of emotion.

The gentlemen were so intent on discussing this interesting secret that they failed to observe Miss Judson looked close to asphyxiation. When she regained her wits, she listened to what the gentlemen were saying.

"What you must do is get up a party of searchers," Joseph suggested. "It's pretty clear he's come to harm. French spies, I expect. I hope they haven't spirited him off to France."

"But how did the French discover who he is?" Vulch asked.

"You may be sure there are villagers in their pay."

"Damme, the villagers didn't know."

"Perhaps some spies followed him from London. Yes, I rather expect that's the way of it," Joseph decided. "And that's what happened to your cargo, Vulch. I never thought Lord Edwin had a thing to do with it. Why, it's infamous, accusing my cousin of thievery. He wouldn't have the wits . . ."

He intercepted a killing glare from Mary Anne and fell silent.

"I did think the project a bit beyond him," Vulch said. He didn't happen to notice Mary Anne's expression.

"What is to be done, then?" Joseph demanded.

"Let us get our heads together and make up a plan. We might as well use the Hall—I'm sure Miss Judson won't mind?"

"Oh—would it not be better to go into town and get the constable's help?" she asked nervously.

"Help? Ha, it's news to me if old Duff Evans has a sane thought in his head," Vulch told her, and strode briskly into the house.

They hadn't been seated in the saloon a moment when Mary Anne heard an earsplitting shriek from the kitchen. In her heart she knew what had caused it. Mr. Robertson, no, Lord Dicaire, had escaped and was coming to arrest her. She froze to the floor.

Chapter Fourteen

"Plummer having a fit of the vapors. She probably saw a mouse," Joseph said.

As no sounds of violence followed the one shriek, Mary Anne had some hope he was correct. Mr. Robertson—she still thought of him as Mr. Robertson—wouldn't have wasted an instant. He would be in the saloon by now, demanding justice, if he had contrived to escape. But her nerves were raw from her ordeal and she had to be sure.

"I'd best just see if Mrs. Plummer is all right," she said, and excused herself. "Would you gentlemen care for some coffee?" she asked before leaving.

"That would be fine, my dear." Vulch nodded.

She got no farther than the top of the kitchen stairs when Mrs. Plummer's head peered up through the door. "Sorry if I disturbed you, Miss Judson. 'Twas only the mouse," she said.

"Good. Could we have coffee for three, please, in the saloon? And if Fitch comes back, tell him Vulch and Joseph are here." She ran back to the saloon to overhear plans for finding the prisoner who was tied up in the basement of the very house that was headquarters for the search.

Mrs. Plummer closed the staircase door and turned back

145

to face Mr. Robertson, who stood across the room with a pistol aimed at her. "I done what you told me, may God forgive me for a coward. You scared the daylights out of me when you popped up them stairs. They never told me you were there." Her eyes slid to her butcher knife, which, unfortunately, rested six inches from the erstwhile prisoner's hand, six feet from her own.

"It won't be necessary to carve me up, Mrs.—Plummer, is it, that Miss Judson called you?" He stuck the pistol in his pocket.

"That's my name, always has been," she allowed. The fellow didn't look such a bloodthirsty customer at close range. He was polite and all.

"I just want to ask you a few questions, then I'll leave. Perhaps you could brush my jacket while we talk?" he suggested.

Having a service to perform settled Mrs. Plummer's nerves and put her a little at her ease. A man would hardly stab you when you were brushing his jacket for him. She might turn him up sweet and save that old ruin of a Lord Eddie from the gallows.

"Miss Judson is very close to her uncle, I think?"

"Close as inkleweavers. He's been father and mother and best friend to the girl since he brought her here twenty years ago. She worships him like a hero," she said, and went on to relate Mary Anne's oft-told tale of her rescue.

Mr. Robertson nodded and asked a few questions.

"What she sees to love in the old sinner is above and beyond me," she griped. "He doesn't remember she's here half the time. Why, for her past two birthdays he didn't even remember to get her a gift, and she must make do with what Fitch and myself can afford—which isn't much, with dog's years of wages due to us. But he has a kind streak in him, when the humor takes him. Her latest birthday, for instance, he gave her a dandy shawl and took her

146

to Folkestone for the day and dinner at the inn, after I had Fitch kill a chicken and baked her favorite raisin cake and all.'' As she chatted, she attacked the coat with a stiff brush.

"Dinner at the inn—was that, by any chance, the first of May?"

"That it was—the very night you first came here yourself, sir. I mind I served the raisin cake."

"And a very fine cake it was, too." He smiled. The lad had a very civil smile for a draper. "They were in Folkestone that day, you said?"

"In every drapery shop in town, and for all their shopping, he couldn't find gloves to go with the shawl. Mind you, the shawl was more than she ever expected. Such a pretty piece, all embroidered like a picture."

Mr. Robertson's blood quickened with this tale. "In every drapery shop in town" indicated Lord Edwin's efforts to sell the cargo and was of little importance. It was the embroidered shawl that intrigued him. The shawl would, presumably, be in Mary Anne's chamber.

"Here you go," Mrs. Plummer said, and handed him the coat. He slid into it and picked up his wrinkled cravat.

"I'd run upstairs and get you one of Lord Edwin's, but I've got to make coffee for the visitors. If you'd care to wait a minute . . ."

"I shan't put you to so much trouble, Mrs. Plummer. You have been very kind. I know where Lord Edwin's bedchamber is. I'll help myself to a clean cravat. Could you spare a little of that hot water to allow me to shave?"

Her tactic was to treat Mr. Robertson like a guest, to reinforce her innocence of any havey-cavey goings-on, and by this time she had almost forgotten he wasn't. She poured out a basin of hot water, and Mr. Robertson went up the servants' stairs to avoid the company. Mrs. Plummer wanted to warn Mary Anne, but knew she couldn't do it with Vulch in the house.

Before going for his shave, Mr. Robertson went into Mary Anne's room and looked all round.

He smiled thoughtfully at its pretty innocence. She and Mrs. Plummer had contrived some thrifty efforts at beautification. There was a dimity canopy on her bed, dyed blue to match the curtains and edged with eyelet. A braided rug was between the bed and the window. He walked to her dresser, noticing its lack of any cosmetics. A somewhat garish gilt dresser set, the gilt worn away to show the white metal beneath, he rightly assigned as an inheritance from her mama. On the dresser sat two miniatures, one of a dark-haired lady who rather resembled Mary Anne, the other of Lord Edwin. Her new dairy was on the bedside table. He damped down the urge to open it and read her outpourings. Morals aside, he had to get on to see the shawl.

It hung in the clothespress, carefully arrayed over the shoulders of a blue silk gown. He laid it flat on the bed and studied the pattern. Unthinkingly he reached for pen and paper. A patent pen sat beside the diary, which was the only writing paper easily available. He removed a blank page and studied the embroidery for several minutes, noting stitch and color, and jotted down notes. When he was satisfied that he had interpreted it properly, he took the shawl and folded it into a small square, which he took to Lord Edwin's room while he shaved.

When he bore some resemblance to the elegant gentleman who had first called at Horton Hall, he returned to Plummer's kitchen and asked for wrapping paper. From the corner of her eye, Plummer saw what it was he was wrapping.

"What are you taking that for?" she demanded suspiciously.

"I'm afraid it's part of the stolen cargo of silk, ma'am. I'll need it for evidence."

Plummer's heart went into nervous palpitations. Evidence—he was gathering evidence against them, after grinning as if butter wouldn't melt in his mouth.

Then Mr. Robertson took up his parcel and left, after politely thanking her for her help. He left by the back door. Mrs. Plummer, uncertain what she should do, knew that informing missie of the man's escape was her top priority. She scribbled up a note and put it on the tray under the coffeepot. She hoped missie didn't scald herself when she saw it. "Robertson's escaped" was all she took time to write.

Lord Dicaire went immediately to the stable and saddled up the mount hired from the inn, safely stowed his parcel in the saddlebag, and left. As he went toward the road, he noticed the mounts tethered under the copper beech in front of the Hall. Vulch's gelding was recognized at once, and while he didn't recognize Joseph's white mare, he knew Miss Judson was sustaining an unwelcome visit from two callers. The poor girl must be on nettles, fearing her fate. It would be cruel to make her wait and wonder all day. With a smile not totally devoid of mischief, he tethered his mount with the others and strode to the Hall.

"Another caller! Who can that be?" Mary Anne exclaimed when the knocker sounded ten seconds later.

She fully expected it would be some officials from London, asking unanswerable questions. They would have been quite welcome as a replacement for who was there—Lord Dicaire. She stared, unable to speak for the dryness of her throat. He had not only escaped, he had managed to make a fresh toilette.

"Good morning, Miss Judson." He smiled impishly. "I was just passing and noticed Mr. Vulch's mount out front. Might I have a word with him? I fear he may be worried at my prolonged absence."

Her hands went out to him in silent supplication. He seized them and fought down the urge to kiss her. "Don't worry. I shan't give you away," he whispered, and walked into the saloon.

"Mr. Robertson!" Vulch exclaimed.

Joseph said "Lord Dicaire!" but in the general melee, the slip went unnoticed.

"Where have you been all night? What happened to you? I was afraid you'd gotten yourself killed!" Vulch said.

"I'm dreadfully sorry. I was unavoidably detained," Lord Dicaire replied. "I received a tip about the silk and had to follow it up. You understand—the less said, the better."

Mary Anne stood like a ghost, listening, while her heart pounded and her mind raced with thoughts of escape.

"I'm off to London at once," Lord Dicaire said, not a moment after his arrival.

"But did you find it?" Vulch asked. "Did you manage to get hold of the, er, the silk?"

"I did. It's all taken care of. I'll speak to Codey before leaving. I'll be in touch, Mr. Vulch." As he went toward the door, Mary Anne followed him.

"How did you escape?" she asked.

"Why, after you so kindly loosened my binding, a friendly mouse completed the job.. Sorry to run off so precipitately, Miss Judson. But then, I fancy you're happy to see the end of me. Pity it isn't the end. I shall be back sooner than you think. Good day."

With a laughing look, he walked out the door, hopped on his mount, and galloped away.

She was certain he was going to call for recruits. He had admitted he was going to speak to Codey. There wasn't a minute to waste. She had to warn Uncle and get away. At this crucial moment, Mrs. Plummer arrived with the coffee tray. Her bulging eyes hinted at all manner of menacing disclosures she wished to make but could not with company present. She gave two or three important looks at the edge of paper protruding below the coffeepot and left.

The two unwelcome callers had only a quick cup of coffee for politeness's sake. Mary Anne read the note but didn't faint or scald herself, as she already knew Robertson had escaped. Vulch was eager to get home and tell his wife that Robertson was a lord, and Joseph wanted to accompany him, to let Bess know Lord Dicarie was not a gentleman whom she had any hope of attaching.

As soon as they were gone, Mary Anne tore down to the kitchen. "What are we going to do? He's gone off to report us, Mrs. Plummer, and Uncle not even home. Oh, we shall all end up on the gibbet, I know it. He said we hadn't seen the last of him."

"He seemed like such a nice lad, too, at first," Mrs. Plummer said, with a wise nod that said she had been disabused of this notion.

"I should never have loosened the binding on his hands. That's what did the mischief. It's all my fault. I was only trying to be kind to him. Fitch had tied them so tightly."

"I ought to warn you, missie, he's been upstairs collecting evidence against you. The shawl your uncle gave you for your birthday—he said it was part of the stolen goods and took it away with him."

"He took my shawl!"

"That he did, as it was part of the stolen cargo," Mrs. Plummer told her regretfully. "I wondered how Lord Edwin managed to pay for it."

"Mrs. Plummer, you've got to take the gig into town

and find Uncle. Tell him what happened. I'll pack up a few necessities for Uncle and myself. We have to escape."

"That's a fool's errand, and you know it. You can't escape the law. The thing to do is get in touch with Lord Exholme."

"Much good that would do us, with Lord Dicaire yelping at our heels. He is a more highly connected gentleman than Exholme."

"Lord Dicaire—that's the fellow that had my kitchen searched."

"That is also Mr. Robertson!"

"Eh?"

"They're one and the same man, Mrs. Plummer."

Mrs. Plummer slapped her cheek. "Then we're done for."

"I know, but we must try. Please do as I say."

Mary Anne went upstairs and hauled the cane case out form the spare room. She hastily grabbed up her linens and a few gowns and threw them in. Then she went into Uncle's room, where she saw the basin of water and razor. So this was where Lord Dicaire had made his toilette. Pretty cool, stepping upstairs for a shave before leaving. He'd been in her room, too—to get his "evidence" against them. She went back to her room, wincing at its rusticity. Lord Dicaire probably lived in a castle.

Then her eyes fell on the bed, where her diary and pen had been cast aside in his hurry. He had even read her diary! The man was an ogre! She blushed at the secrets it held. Her girlish outpourings about meeting him. How he must have laughed! Then she quickly reviewed whether she had mentioned the stolen silk. No, she hadn't written anything last night. That was why he hadn't he taken it for more evidence. She stuffed it into the suitcase and closed the fastening. She didn't like to go into Fitch's room. He could add his few necessities when they got back.

When the suitcase was packed, there was nothing to do but wait. She made a slow tour of her favorite rooms, remembering a hundred, a thousand, pleasant times. Christmas in the dining room, with suckling pig and plum pudding. Long and lovely idle evenings in the study, browsing through Uncle's ancient tomes while he glanced through month-old journals, and the wind whistled outside, stirring the dark curtains. He used to drink brandy—"my medicine" he called it, when she was young.

Uncle's study, where he tried to teach her to read and cipher, and had given up when he discovered he couldn't do long division himself. It must have strained his thin purse to provide her lessons in the village with Bess Vulch, but he had done it, insisted on paying his share of the tutor's fee, though not always on time.

She heard the rattle of the front door and dashed out to meet Uncle as he came in with Fitch and Mrs. Plummer.

"We're ditched," Lord Edwin said. "Missie, you're going to Exholme's place. They won't dare go after you there."

"We're all going," she announced calmly. "I've already packed. Fitch, you must gather up your own things. Will you come with us, Mrs. Plummer, or stay behind?"

"I'm going with you, to Lord Exholme's. We decided it between us, missie. It's for the best. There's no reason you should hang with Lord Edwin and Fitch. This imbroglio wasn't your doing," she said with a fierce eye at the perpetrators.

"Not one step shall I stir without Uncle," Mary Anne insisted.

"I can't go," Lord Edwin explained. "They must have someone to hang, but there's no reason for us all to die.

153

I've persuaded Fitch he must drive the carriage, and I shall stay behind to accept full responsibility." For the first time in his life he was accepting responsibility for his deeds, and no one noticed, not even he himself. His main sensation was annoyance that Mary Anne insisted on arguing.

"No!" Mary Anne said firmly. "We all stay or we all go. It's up to you, Uncle."

He held his grizzled head in his hands and moaned. "Oh, why is everyone so impossible? Robertson turning into a lord before our very eyes and abusing my hospitality in this underbred manner. If he's a lord, why can't he behave like one? I never wanted him here. He insisted on staying. Why didn't he escape last night, before we had to bring him to the Hall? I never gave that order, Fitch. That was your doing."

"I couldn't leave him in the barn, in case Codey came by."

"Codey—there is another thorn in my side. No doubt he's at the barn stealing my silk, after all the trouble I went to to get it from the Frenchies."

"Stealing from the Frenchies shouldn't be a crime," Mrs. Plummer stated. "Not when they were such gossoons as to run away and abandon the ship. Why, anyone with a wit in his head would know enough to salvage it."

Lord Edwin cast a questioning eye at her. The words "abandon the ship," and especially "salvage," stirred dim memories of his days at Whitehall.

"I daresay a good, sharp lawyer could get me off," he said thoughtfully. Mary Anne saw his fingers begin to tap his cheek, and she looked hopeful.

Fitch, whose mind moved more slowly, said, "You're wiser to stay away from lawyers. You'll be bitten to death by their fees."

"There is something in marine law about the cargo of an abandoned ship being fair game for salvagers," Lord

Edwin said. "I heard some such thing when I was with the Admiralty. There's another point in my defense—my illustrious career with the Admiralty. Why, between that and a man's patriotic duty in outwitting the French and my having only salvaged goods from an abandoned ship, they haven't a leg to stand on. And there's habeas corpus," he added, his mind going astray. "Cui bono—yes, indeed. I may sue them for false arrest and make a bundle of blunt. You'd best take a run down to the barn and scare Codey away if he's there, Fitch. And make sure Belle don't climb up to the loft and eat the rest of the stuff."

Fitch left, and Mary Anne continued her persuasions that they leave immediately. "I'll just have a look in my library," Lord Edwin said. "I'm quite certain a man may take goods from an abandoned ship. A derelict ship, I believe, is the legal term. Wine, Plummer. I shall need a deal of wine to sort this out. *In vino veritas*, eh, what?"

"Bring him coffee," Mary Anne said. In this minor matter, at least, she had her way.

She went with her uncle to the library to thumb through the dusty tomes, looking for a way out of their problem, but in her heart she knew the only hope of escaping the gibbet was to flee.

"Ah, here we are!" Lord Edwin exclaimed, fingering a page in one of his books and laughing gleefully.

"What is it, Uncle?"

"Hmm," he said, happily tapping his cheek. "I shall be with you shortly, my dear. This is very interesting. Most interesting. A derelict, yes, certainly it was abandoned. 'Provision extends to a British ship anywhere in the world and foreign ships in British waters.' Yes, certainly it was in British waters. If my bit of bay ain't British waters, I should like to know what is. And there wasn't a soul aboard. Abandoned is what it was. No question."

"What have you found?" she repeated.

"Pour me a fresh cup of coffee, will you?" he said, and handed her his cup, without taking his nose from the book.

After reading for several minutes, with many gurgles of self-congratulation, Lord Edwin looked up and smiled benignly. "What you are looking at, my dear, is a salvor. That's a chap who saves goods off a ship. A derelict ship, which that French lugger certainly was, is fair game for all comers. The owner may reclaim his property by coming forward, but I shouldn't think we need fear the Frenchies will step forward and announce what they were up to, eh? Not if they know what's good for them. Mind you, there are a few fine points I shall have to take up with my lawyer. Something about a derelict being a ship 'without hope of recovery or intention of returning to it' by the owners. But in the worst case, I am owed salvage money. As the salvor, I need not return the cargo till my claim is satisfied. I have a legal lien on the stuff. I may institute legal proceedings in rem against the property."

"What does that mean—'in rem'?"

"How the deuce should I know? This salvage money—very interesting. Not an exact formula, it depends on many factors. The labor expended, for instance. We busted our backs, Fitch and I, getting the stuff ashore. And just look at all the labor expended since then in keeping it safe. Skill and promptitude displayed—ho, it was a pretty skillful piece of work, I can tell you, and prompt, too. I was out of bed and into my inexpressibles in jig time. As to the degree of danger—why, we've had half the county chasing us, to say nothing of drinking poisoned wine."

"It might be best to omit your effort to put Lord Dicaire to sleep, Uncle. Would all this apply to smuggled goods, and in war time?"

"Even more so," he said confidently. "I'll have my lawyer look into it."

"There's still the matter of having kidnapped Lord Dicaire and the secret message. That puts a different complexion on it.''

"Who?''

"Mr. Robertson. He is Lord Dicaire. Didn't Plummer tell you?''

"Yes, she mentioned some such thing. I never heard of Lord Dicaire.''

"You might know his papa, Lord Pelham.''

"You never mean it! Not Peachie's lad? He don't look a thing like his da. Why, I have know his papa forever. We were at school together. I think we are some kind of cousin—that wretched remove kind that only maiden aunts can figure out. Why, Peachie would never let his lad prosecute me. Ho, my dear, what we have been involved in here is a comedy of errors. Much ado about nothing. But all's well that ends well, eh, what? I haven't time to chat about Shakespeare now, my dear. I must run into town and speak to my lawyer. Who is my lawyer, Mary Anne? I seem to have forgotten his name.''

"You don't have one, Uncle, but Mr. Hawken is considered the best lawyer in these parts.''

"Oh, quite, a sterling chap! I shall visit Mr. Hawken.''

"I think it would be better if we left,'' she insisted.

"By all means, you and Plummer run along to my brother's place, but not till I am back from town. I won't have you landing in on Bertie in a gig. He likes to throw in my face that I live on a bone here at the Hall. Whose fault is that, I should like to know! And put on that new shawl I gave you—ah! Heh, heh, Plummer tells me you have learned my little trick. I shall get it back for you, never fear. I shall insist on it as part of my compensation. There is no fixed formula. I shall demand your shawl back. I would have bought you one, but the old pockets were to let.''

She smiled at his foolishness. Dear Uncle. She wouldn't

go to Lord Exholme's mansion, not if it meant facing Lord Dicaire and a whole jury. Her uncle needed her here. She had somewhat less confidence than her uncle that he was a salvor. What he was was a thief, but such a lovable thief that she forgave him.

Chapter Fifteen

While Mary Anne worried and fretted and continued laying plans to escape if necessary, Lord Edwin tootled merrily into Dymchurch to call on Mr. Hawken, who greeted him with a very civil curiosity.

"What can I do for you today, Lord Edwin?" he asked.

Lord Edwin regarded Mr. Hawken and decided the man was to be trusted. He had a good honest figure, slightly paunchy. There was none of that "yon Cassius" leanness about him that could suggest a hunger for undue profit. He had frank blue eyes, and best of all, he didn't work for Vulch.

"I am here on a matter of the gravest importance, sir," Lord Edwin said, his little chest swollen with significance. "National importance, in fact."

"Ah, I didn't realize you still worked for the Admiralty."

"Only informally now. Perhaps you would just close that door, Mr. Hawken. I see your clerk lurking about with his ears stretched." Mr. Hawken closed the door. "And perhaps the window—anyone might be listening in from the street." Whether someone could hear anything from a second-story window was a moot point in Mr. Hawken's estimation, but he closed the window.

When they were hermetically sealed in the office, Lord Edwin opened his budget, and Mr. Hawken heard a tale that left him wondering whether to laugh or to worry. Being a man of sound common sense, he had soon discovered the truth beneath the layers of rodomontade. Old Lord Eddie had snitched Vulch's cargo, and by God, he just might get away with it, if young Dicaire didn't kick up a dust.

"It's a highly unusual case," Mr. Hawken said. "I've handled several salvage cases, of course, here on the coast, but this one has unique features. The ship was abandoned, but whether it would qualify as a derelict so close to shore raises severe doubts. On the other hand, Vulch got the ship freed by claiming it was a fishing vessel, so they can hardly come forward now and claim it was anything else. Fishing vessels don't carry a hold full of silk."

"Prima facie evidence." Lord Edwin nodded sagely.

"As to the matter of national importance you mention—something to do with delivering secret messages out of France, I assume—the government will hardly want to advertise that, either."

"Don't breathe a world of that, Mr. Hawken, I pray. Ah, and did I mention that the Admiralty man on the case is kin to me? Yes, the son of my cousin and good friend. His papa won't let him make any trouble. I fancy there may be a little something brewing between the fellow and my niece as well. He rescued her from the Frenchies, quite the young gallant. I see him rolling his eyes at her, you know, when he thinks no one is looking. A whiff of April and May in the air."

"I'll get straight into my book of precedents and see what I can come up with, but between you and me and the bedpost, Lord Edwin, I doubt this will ever come to court. And it is best for you that it not do so. I suggest you hide the silk from Vulch till you can dispose of it, but

160

that is not professional legal advice, mind. Just between neighbors. I fancy no more will be said on the matter.''

Lord Edwin smiled happily, shook Mr. Hawken's hand, and said he would be looking forward to receiving his bill. By the living jingo, he might even pay it, if all went well. An excellent chap, Mr. Hawken.

After enjoining his solicitor to the greatest secrecy, Lord Edwin dashed into the street and told everyone he met that he couldn't stop to talk as he was involved in a most important matter. This naturally elicited the question, ''What is this matter, Lord Edwin?'' and with no further urging, he told the whole, only refraining from mentioning that there was a secret message in the cargo.

''I pulled a sly one on the Frenchies,'' he whispered behind raised fingers. ''Got away with their last cargo—that's a thousand guineas that won't go into Boney's coffers.''

''Nor Vulch's, either,'' one of his friends said, smiling. Mr. Vulch was successful enough to be resented. ''What you ought to do is speak to Miss Delancey at the drapery shop about selling the stuff. Is it good quality?''

''The very finest.''

Miss Delancey would be *aux anges* to get it, no doubt, and it would save Fitch a trip to Folkestone. Lord Edwin paid a reconnaissance trip to Miss Delancey, whose shelves of silk were wonderfully thin, and left her in hope of seeing them full by morning.

''Vulch always brings the stuff at midnight—the back door,'' Miss Delancey told him. ''This evening is a good time for it. The spring assembly will take care of Codey. He never misses it. I shall leave the assembly at eleven-thirty and be at the back door of the shop to check the merchandise.'' The Dymchurch assemblies were no top-lofty affairs. Merchants and revenue men were allowed to

161

become genteel for the evening, or the hall would have been three-quarters empty.

"And I shall check your coin, madame," Lord Edwin replied smartly. Demmed merchants, all alike. A very toplofty way they had about them.

Of Lord Dicaire there was not a trace in the village. Lord Edwin met Vulch, who had gotten wind of the story and had gone looking for him.

"Now, see here, Lord Eddie. I know perfectly well you've stolen my goods, and I mean to have them back."

"Stolen?" Lord Edwin asked, assuming his stiffest face, which resembled a wounded hound. "Are you referring to the salvage operation I executed on the derelict vessel in front of my place on the first of May? If you wish to step forward and claim ownership of that contraband, sir, I shall be quite satisfied with the salvage award. You may speak to my solicitor, Mr. Hawken. He is representing my interests in this legal matter." Joyful words! His lowly theft had risen to a perfectly respectable legal matter.

"Lord Dicaire will have something to say about that! There was more than silk involved, as I fancy you know pretty well!

"Mr. Vulch!" he exclaimed, nearly bursting with indignation and looking over his shoulder for eavesdroppers. "Is this your idea of national security, to be shouting on the street corners what else was in that cargo? The Admiralty will have to find another liaison man, if *this* is your notion of security."

Vulch paced swiftly to his solicitor, who advised him to drop the matter entirely. "You'll look nohow, Adrian. The thing is done. Best lay off, or Lord Eddie might manage to pull the whole business out from under you. He has friends in high places and a shore as conveniently placed as your own."

"By God, that's what he's up to, the sly weasel!"

This possibility had already occurred to the sly weasel, only to be abandoned. It was a deuced nuisance. If it weren't for the thousand guineas to be collected from Miss Delancey that evening, he would regret ever having become involved in it. With trips to Folkestone and having to get out of bed at midnight in a storm and deal with merchants and smugglers, a man would have to be very fond of gold to put himself to so much trouble.

When he had exhausted all the entertainment value in the affair, Lord Edwin had lunch at the inn and finally, around three o'clock in the afternoon, returned to the Hall. His niece met him, her face pinched with worry and her spirits worn to a thread.

"What has kept you so long, Uncle? I was afraid you'd been arrested. What had Mr. Hawken to say?"

"Smooth sailing, my dear. Much ado about nothing. We can talk about Shakespeare now, if you like."

"I would rather talk about escape. If we—"

"Escape? Why, what put such a silly bee in your bonnet? I thought I would find your hair in rags and your face covered in lotion for the assembly this evening. I must attend the assembly; I have business to execute."

"We daren't go!"

"Rubbish. I must be there. But I shall have to leave a little early, about eleven forty-five should do it. I'll return and pick you up later."

"Uncle—has this 'business' something to do with the silk?"

"Nonsense. That is all taken care of, my pet. What a worrywart you are, filling my head with fears for nothing. Mr. Hawken says there is nothing to worry about."

"But Lord Dicaire took the shawl as evidence."

"Ha, we've heard the last of that sort of thing. They'll sweep it all under the carpet, according to Hawken. No alternative, really. Whitehall don't want their stories bandied about the countryside. And if they go producing evidence, we have prima facie evidence on our side. The best sort. Now go and twist your hair up in rags, or you'll look a quiz at the party.''

''Are you sure?''

''Of course I'm sure. A pity your beau won't be there.''

''Is Joseph not attending?'' she asked hopefully.

''Joseph? I hope you don't think I mean that scarecrow! I am speaking of Peachie's son, Lord Dicaire. I know what is afoot. I ain't blind, you know. Romeo and Juliet! Ha, yes, indeed. All's well that ends well. As you like it, what?''

''Lord Dicaire is not my beau!'' she exclaimed. ''Did you see him in town?''

''He's gone to London. My old friends at the Admiralty will set him straight if his papa don't.''

With Lord Dicaire safely in London, and with her uncle assuring her the matter was solved, Mary Anne's thoughts turned to the assembly. It was the social event of the year. She hated to miss it. Why not go?

''What had Vulch to say to all this? Did you see him?''

''Poor Vulch!'' Lord Edwin laughed. ''He went tearing off like a jackrabbit. I put the fear of God into him, with his loose tongue. Now, don't look aghast, my dear. Just go and twist your hair up in rags. You want to be in top form for the little jig this evening.''

Mary Anne went to her room and applied the strips of rag to her hair. She had some natural curl, but for balls she usually put in the rags to give it additional bounce. Her mind was all in a whirl. That morning she had thought her world was coming to an end. All of a sudden the matter was miraculously solved. The lost message was a secret, so legal steps would not be taken to punish them for losing it. Vulch was in retreat; Lord Dicaire had gone off to London. He had said he would be back, but he would have to ride nonstop to be back before the ball was over, so she should be safe for tonight.

She put some hope in her uncle's relationship with Lord Dicaire's father. And in a pinch, there was always Lord Edwin's brother. Exholme was a gentleman of some importance in London. Very likely they would escape the gibbet, but her happiness was far from complete. She wouldn't be waltzing with Mr. Robertson. There was no Mr. Robertson, only Lord Dicaire, who was a different thing entirely.

Uncle might harbor some fond ideas about creating a match between them, but she knew well enough that eminent peers did not marry penniless orphans. They married heiresses with names like Lady Arabella of Cholomondey Hall or The Honorable Miss Montagu of Hinton Castle. They certainly didn't marry ladies who kidnapped them and locked them in barns and dank cellars. These were her thoughts while her uncle went in search of Fitch.

He found him at the barn, resting in a stack of hay, while Belle stolidly nibbled at the barn door. "Well, lazybones," Lord Edwin said merrily, "this is how you slave when I'm not here to keep an eye on you, eh? Reclining like an odalisque on her divan. Excellent news, Fitch."

Fitch sat up. "What's that, then?"

"I've found a buyer, right in Dymchurch," he said, and outlined his clever day's work.

"How am I to get the stuff to Delancey's back door?" Fitch inquired. "You'll be using the carriage for the spring assembly. Jeremy won't lend me his boat again."

"There's the gig . . ."

"Carry the stuff along the public roads in an open gig—right into town? And it would take a few trips."

"Hmm, I see your problem, Fitch. What you'll have to do is drive us to the assembly hall and come back. Delan-

165

cey don't want the stuff till midnight. You'll have plenty of time to get the silk into town in the carriage.''

"It'll take three or four trips, and what am I to do with the first loads while I go for the others? I can't leave them in Delancey's back alley for someone to make off with. You'll have to leave the assembly and stand guard at the shop.''

Lord Edwin had looked forward to the assembly with particular relish. He recognized himself for a hero if no one else did and expected a busy round of congratulations. Then, too, there was Vulch, to be smirked at throughout the night.

"Impossible. It would look suspicious if I were to leave the assembly.''

"Then it can't be done,'' Fitch told him.

"Can't? How easily you fellows give up. You'd never pass muster at the Admiralty, my lad. There must be some solution. Ah, I have it. The hay wain. No one suspected it the first time we used it. We'll hide the cargo under a few bits of straw and you can take it all to town in one load.''

"That hay wain don't move, Lord Eddie. It's been there since the Ice Age. It would fall apart if you tried to move it. And it only has three wheels.''

"You couldn't hammer a wheel on to it—just for one night? An ad hoc wheel, so to speak?''

"There's no wheel to hammer. The gig wheels aren't a quarter of the size. You'd not have time to get one made up. The hay wain won't do.''

"*My* hay wain won't do. That is not to say Joseph's will not do very well. Hop over to Joseph's and borrow his hay wain.''

"It'll look might odd, borrowing a hay wain a month before there's hay to be cut.''

"The perfect time. He can hardly refuse to lend it when

166

he has no use for it. He *will* refuse though, the bounder. Joseph wouldn't lend me the lint off his brush. Don't bother asking him, Fitch. Just take it. He leaves it in his barn. If you go after milking time, there oughtn't to be anyone around to ask questions. Do it right after you deliver Mary Anne and myself to the assembly. Well, that's settled, then. Now you can get back to your rest.''

Fitch scowled to consider his busy evening. ''Them bales are heavy. I've moved them a dozen times already. It seems to me, I ought to get more than a few guineas for all my efforts.''

''You servants are all alike. Lying on your backs all day, thinking of nothing but bilking your employers out of their money. You know I must buy missie some fancy clothes for her trousseau, Fitch. Would you rob the poor gel of her one chance to nab a decent parti?''

''Eh?'' Fitch asked, staring in disbelief.

''It's as well as settled. Mind you,'' he added, ''Lord Dicaire is well inlaid. He might pay for the trousseau himself. Then you and I will be high in the stirrups. I'm thinking of buying a new team, Fitch. How would you like that, eh? And you can be my groom—my chief groom.''

''With a proper groom's outfit?''

''Anything you fancy, Fitch. We'll run up to London and visit Tattersall's.''

''Stay at a hotel?''

''The very finest. But first you must get that load into Dymchurch. Make sure you sprinkle a little hay over the bales, in case anyone takes a look. Miss Judson and I will need the carriage at seven-thirty. I want you shaved and in a decent jacket, Fitch. The whole town will be attending the assembly. We must arrive in the highest kick of fashion. Give the carriage a wash-down, and don't forget to brush the horses. I'll see if Plummer can get the spots out of my monkey suit. Heigh-ho, I'm off.''

Chapter Sixteen

Fitch was as spruce as Plummer's brush and iron could make him when he pulled the carriage up to the front door of the Hall for Lord Edwin and Mary Anne to enter. The ancient carriage could not be said to shine, but its fading paint glowed dully from Fitch's exertions. The team pulling it didn't shine, either, but the dust and hay had been removed from their coats, rendering them passable in the fading light of day.

Lord Edwin smiled with satisfaction, seeing not the results of Fitch's labor but the new team that would soon stand in the harness. Matched bays is what he wanted, with a white blaze on the forehead. He offered his arm to his niece and they entered the carriage.

Why Mary Anne chose this wonderful night to fall into the sullens was a mystery to her uncle. She looked fine as ninepence in her best blue silk. No doubt it was losing her shawl that put that droop to her lips.

"I'll replace it, my dear, never fear," he said.

"Replace what, Uncle?"

"Your shawl. I told you, I'll buy you a new one, and Plummer can stitch some gewgaws on it, like the one Dicaire took to London."

The mention of Dicaire only dragged her lips lower.

"You need not do that. My white shawl is fine." She drew it more closely around her shoulders as she spoke.

"I don't know what's the matter with everybody today," Lord Edwin said in exasperation. "Fitch as surly as a bear, demanding money from me for sitting on his haunches all day. My niece pouting because she lost a stupid shawl. And Plummer! I swear she burned that fish pie on purpose."

Mary Anne made an effort to simulate good spirits for the remainder of the trip. Once they actually arrived, the distraction of the assembly revived her. She admired the bunting, left over from the Prince of Wales's visit five years before, that was always strung along the walls for special occasions. The paper flowers attached to it lent a festive touch. There were all the ladies' toilettes to be scanned, a quick search of the crowd to see if anyone had an interesting visitor who had been brought along to the party. Some years, folks drove in from as far as ten miles away, to create a little interest. There now, who was that rather handsome fellow with the Bentleys? She'd never seen him before. Soon she spotted the Vulches and waved to Bess.

Bess, of course, had a smart new gown, with just half a dozen or so too many bows for real elegance. The paisley shawl was a trifle loud with her blue-and-white-striped gown, but really, she looked very pretty when she came forward, smiling.

"My, don't you look fine, Mary Anne. Your blue gown never looked better. I thought we would see the new shawl your uncle gave your for your birthday."

"It didn't match my gown," Mary Anne said. "You look lovely, Bess. Who's the stranger with the Bentleys?"

"Isn't he handsome?" Bess replied, but with no real interest. The reason for it soon came out. "He's married to Mrs. Bentley's sister. His name's Harcourt, an innkeeper from Kingsnorth. I haven't seen Joseph. Is he not coming?"

"I'm sure he'll be here."

"I thought he would come with you," Bess said, casting a curious look at her friend.

"He never comes with us."

Bess gave her a quizzing smile. "You want to look sharp, or someone will steal him from you."

Mary Anne smiled without a single sign of rancor. "I think I know who that someone will be, Bess."

Bess colored up prettily and found it was time to change the subject. She mentioned one dear to Mary Anne's heart, despite the pain it caused. "A pity Lord Dicaire could not stay for the assembly. Imagine, Mary Anne—a viscount, and we not knowing a thing about it. Mama is sorry she didn't do more entertaining while he was with us. She didn't use half the silver, either. We nearly swooned when we learned who he was. Joseph says he has the highest instep in the Western Hemisphere. He never associates with any but the tip of the ton in London."

"Will he be returning?" Mary Anne asked, and looked across the room, as though only half listening.

"I shouldn't think so. Oh, look, here is Joseph arriving. I'll call him, shall I? He'll want to have the first dance with you."

"No, please!"

She waved. Joseph advanced at a hot pace, and when he was nearly there, spotted Mary Anne standing beside Bess. A fine predicament! The fiddlers were tuning up; gentlemen were choosing partners. He must offend either the girl he felt he ought to marry or the one he wanted to.

His mama saw his dilemma at once and rushed to his rescue. "Mary Anne. You haven't been to call on me this spring, naughty girl," she said, and took her arm to lead her away. "Where is your uncle? Take me to him. I want to speak to him about the strange stories I hear circulating. He got hold of Vulch's silk, did he? Fancy Bess still speaking to you.'' On a string of pleasantries she walked a very relieved Mary Anne away from Joseph and Bess.

"Ah, here is Sir Lyle Skate looking for a partner," Mrs. Horton exclaimed when this gentleman happened by. "You are in luck, sir." She smiled and handed over Mary Anne. "I see Lord Eddie over by the punch bowl." Where else? "I'll speak to him."

Mary Anne took her place beside Sir Lyle for the opening minuet. She suffered no lack of partners. Joseph Horton claimed her for the second dance and scolded her for running off just as he was about to ask her for the first one.

"I had to ask Bess, for the looks of it," he said defensively.

"Cut line, Joseph," she said sharply. Her nerves were taut from the day's exacerbation. "You know perfectly well you want to marry her, and she wants to marry you. You don't have to apologize to me for it. I think it an excellent match. With her money and your respectability, you may fly as high as you both want."

"It never entered my mind!"

"It entered your heart, I think, and Bess's, too. That's the way folks should marry."

Joseph was elated to hear so much common sense from her. "And what rich commoner do you have in your eyes?" he teased.

Her card was full to intermission, but the party held no real pleasure for her. She knew it was impossible that Lord Dicaire's broad shoulders should appear at the doorway, yet she found her eyes turning in that direction ten times during every dance.

She received a deal of good-natured teasing about her uncle's prank. That, at least, seemed to have dwindled to a joke, but there was still Dicaire's rough treatment at her uncle's hands to worry about. She didn't think he'd let that matter drop. "I shall be back sooner than you think," he had said. His return could only spell trouble, yet she looked once more, eagerly, to the door, only to see Uncle in deep conversation with Miss Delancey. It was eleven-thirty. Just one more set before the midnight supper was to be served. She had refused two invitations to join other parties for the supper, thinking to sit with her uncle.

While Mary Anne frolicked through a country dance, Lord Edwin slipped quietly out, ostensibly to blow a cloud, but in reality to dart off to Delancey's Drapery Shop. The exchange went off without a hitch. Miss Delancey had her gig waiting, and was back at the assembly hall before the first course was over.

Lord Edwin remained behind to have a few words with Fitch. "A good night's work, lad," he said, and handed Fitch his three guineas. "Now it remains only for you to get Joseph's hay wain back before it's missed and clean yourself up to bring us the carriage to return home after the assembly."

"Couldn't you get a lift home with Joseph?" Fitch asked. His big shoulders ached. He was hot and tired, and most of all, he had a thirst to match his size. The tavern was only a block away, and he had the unaccustomed pleasure of coins jingling in his pockets.

"That jackdaw? He'll be drooling all over Mary Anne's best gown if we get in his carriage. You've done such a fine job of polishing up my rig that I want to show off your work, Fitch. Two o'clock should be early enough. They have another round of jigging after the dinner. If you look lively, you can make it. I'm off. I smelled goose tarts coming out of the kitchen. Heigh-ho."

Fitch wiped his brow and sighed. He thought of a tall glass of ale, all foaming on top, the way they served it at the tavern. He had time for one glass, if he hurried. Lord Eddie was sitting down to a fine dinner. He deserved a glass of ale, demmed if he didn't.

When midnight arrived and Lord Edwin was not to be found, Mary Anne stood, looking for some friendly party she could attach herself to. She would join Bess, except that Joseph was stuck to her arm like a burr. They'd be eating with Vulch and his wife, and really, she disliked to intrude there so soon after Uncle's prank.

Bess spotted her and came darting over. "My dear, are you all alone? You must join us. No one asked poor Mary Anne to dinner, Joseph," she explained aside in a perfectly carrying voice. "Tell her she must join us."

Joseph offered his arm, and Mary Anne was obliged either to take it or to sit alone. She went along to Vulch's table, where Vulch glowered like a gargoyle and his wife simpered demurely.

"Do try a slice of this chicken, Mary Anne. It was made by our own cook. As tender a bird as ever stepped out of the oven, if I do say so myself."

Lord Edwin had been busy filling the dame's head with some highly imaginative stories of an approaching match between his old friend's son, Lord Dicaire, and Mary Anne. Mrs. Vulch was delighted, as this left Joseph free for her own girl. She had no notion of letting such a prize friend slip through her fingers, either. Lady Dicaire could open doors in London for Joseph and Bess. Bess was in on the story, too, but didn't believe a word of it. No one could bring a gent up to scratch that quickly, especially not a slow top like Mary Anne.

"A pity a certain gentleman had to dart back to London," Mrs. Vulch said archly.

After a frowning pause Mary Anne said, "Do you mean Lord Dicaire?"

"Who else would I be talking about, my dear? A little bird whispered the secret in my ear."

Mary Anne stared in confusion. "What secret is that, ma'am?"

"Why, Miss Judson, I mean your betrothal, to be sure. What a sly boots you are, but as I was just saying to Adrian, still waters run deep."

"Mrs. Vulch, I am not betrothed!" Mary Anne gasped, and looked once more to the door. On this occasion she was highly relieved not to see it full of Dicaire's broad shoulders.

"I understand." Mrs. Vulch nodded, though she didn't understand at all what the secret was. Happen the gent's papa disapproved? "I shan't breathe a whisper of it. When is the big day to be, Miss Judson?"

"Truly, there is nothing between Lord Dicaire and myself. I scarcely know him."

"Ho, and for a near stranger he calls Codey off! Very well, if that's the way it is, you are marrying a stranger, and a mighty eligible one, too, from what Joseph tells us. Very well to grass. His estate has thousands of acres of prime land in Surrey, to say nothing of the London house. Tell me—Adrian wasn't sure—does he have a hunting box in the Cotswold hills as well?"

"I have no idea. Really, I hardly know him."

"There's nothing like connections when all is said and done. Dicaire's papa and Lord Eddie bosom bows, and your uncle never mentioning his name all these years. Imagine catching such a plum for you."

Mrs. Vulch refused to listen to reason. The best Mary Anne could get from her was a promise of silence, which the woman executed at the top of her lungs. That dinner rated as the worst of Mary Anne's life. As though Mrs. Vulch's raucous teasing and Vulch's scowls were not enough, Bess kept sliding those sly glances across the table, mingled with low murmurs to Joseph. Though her words were inaudible, the nature of them was obvious from her smirking smiles.

The dinner was long and seemed interminable. Lord Edwin entered the hall not long after twelve, but he steered a clear path of Vulch and sat with the bachelors, so that Mary Anne couldn't join him. At long last the meats were removed and the sweets were served. Plates of cakes and cream buns, of ices and sorbets, of fruit tarts and candied fruit were brought forth, enough to destroy every tooth in the county. It was Mary Anne's favorite part of the meal, but she looked with no interest at the treats on this occasion. She wanted only to go home.

She cast a pleading look across the hall to her uncle, who was regaling the bachelors with tales of his daring. She looked to the cloak room, wondering how long she could hide out there without attracting attention, and finally she looked with longing to the doorway. She shook her head and looked again. It couldn't be! He couldn't have been to London and back already! It was fifty miles there, a hundred there and back. It was impossible that this perfectly wretched day was to be capped by public disgrace at the hands of Lord Dicaire.

But she knew as surely as she knew he was scanning the hall that it was she he was looking for. From a crouching position behind Joseph's head she peered across the room. There, he had spotted Uncle; he was looking for her. Now his dark head turned to Vulch's table. Oh, God, he was coming! He had seen her. Mrs. Vulch would surely congratulate him on his engagement. She would be the laughingstock of the room. She had to stop him. She pushed her plate back and stood up, her knees trembling.

"Excuse me," she said, and fled across the room to intercept Lord Dicaire. She would hear his charges in private, She could at least spare herself public disgrace.

"I told you so!" Mrs. Vulch called across the table to Bess, who tossed her curls angrily.

"Just look at how she runs after him," Bess pointed out to Joseph.

"Shameless hussy!" Joseph said admiringly.

Chapter Seventeen

Her trip to Dicaire that had begun on a mad dart slowed to near immobility as she drew nearer. Lord Dicaire didn't come to meet her. He was content to let her come to him. She had set out expecting to have her ears scorched, but as she drew near, he put his two hands out to her and smiled softly. She ignored his outstretched hands.

"Why did you come?" she asked in a low whisper.

He observed that there was more fear than joy in her greeting and seized her hands to draw her nearer. "Why, a gentleman always keeps his promises, Mary Anne, and I promised you I would return."

"You didn't say tonight!"

"I decided to leave you in the dark on that score, as you left me in the dark in your cellar."

He folded his arm over hers and patted her hand possessively as he surveyed the throng. Every head in the room was turned to the door. Every eye stared at the elegant gentleman and Miss Judson. The clink of cutlery on crockery and the murmur in the hall fell still.

"Do you think we ought to bow or something?" Lord Dicaire asked, and laughed.

"I think you should be warned," she said, "that Uncle has hired a lawyer. Mr. Hawken feels he has a very good chance of getting him off. Possession is nine-tenths of the law, you know."

"It was certainly nine-tenths of the problem." A smile played in the dark recesses of his eyes. "I consider the matter closed. As to my own incarceration in the cellar, you surely don't imagine I will boast of being bested by a girl and a bruiser? Tell me, what other laws has your uncle been breaking? It can only be of the law of gravity; he's already ruptured all the others."

His speech was delivered in accents more playful than serious, yet more loving than playful. She looked up at him doubtfully through the fan of her long lashes.

Before more was said, Lord Eddie came legging toward them. "So you made it back, eh, Dicaire? Nice to see you again. How is your papa?"

"He was fine, the last I heard."

"Still chasing after the fillies, is he? The two-legged ones, I mean. What a man he was. You don't much resemble your papa in looks."

Mary Anne bit her lips, waiting to hear what insults her uncle was about to deliver on his old friend. "No, sir," Lord Edwin continued. "Your father was a fine figure of a man, and handsome." Rheumy blue eyes skimmed over the well-built Adonis before him. "My own papa was the same, a fine specimen," he said sadly. "The human race is petering out. Here are you and I, sunk to caricatures of our ancestors."

"My father is five feet and eight inches," Lord Dicaire told him.

"Eh, five feet? Why, Peachie was a giant. Built like my Fitch."

"My father's name is Alexander. You must be thinking of someone else."

"Aren't you Lord Peacham's lad?" he demanded.

"No, sir, my father is the Earl of Pelham."

"Pelham, you say? Well, I'll be damned. I thought you was Peachie's son. I made sure of it, or I wouldn't have been in such a hurry to hand over my niece to you."

"Uncle!" Mary Anne exclaimed, horrified, and cast an apologetic smile at Dicaire.

"Too late to shimmy out of it now," Dicaire warned him. "Take care, or I'll have you up on a breach of promise suit."

"I don't mean to say I forbid the match," Lord Eddie said mildly. "You seem a decent sort of lad, but there's Peachie's boy, you see. He is expecting to marry Mary Anne."

"Uncle," Mary Anne said, "there is Mr. Hawken looking for you. You had best speak to him."

"Is he, by Jove? Yes, he will be after his blunt now that I—heh, heh. You youngsters run along, then, but mind you behave yourselves."

Lord Dicaire lifted a questioning brow. "Tell me, when was this match between you and Peacham's son arranged?"

"You would do better to ask where. It was all in Uncle's head. He thought a match between his friend's son and myself would lessen the chance of prosecution."

"I'll bear that in mind."

The youngsters went to a small table in the corner of the room. "What happened in London?" Mary Anne asked. It was not what she wished to discuss, but she was curious.

"We read your shawl and figured out Mrs. Lalonde's message."

"I beg your pardon?"

"Your shawl. Mrs. Lalonde embroiders her messages in silk, in case they are intercepted. It is an old system, resurrected from the medieval ages. Mr. Barton, an antiquarian at the Admiralty, came across the idea. We trained a woman and sent her to France, where she managed to find work in the proper circles. Each stitch has a meaning, each color of silk, and each figure in the pattern.''

"You mean it was my *shawl* you were looking for all the time? I thought it was a piece of paper—a note!''

"I didn't know it was a shawl. Mrs. Lalonde uses various items. If the message is brief, she sometimes uses only a little silk runner or handkerchief, Other times I have received ladies' reticules or gloves.''

"How curious! And you decipher the messages?''

He nodded. "I have it double-checked by Barton, just to be sure. He's the expert.''

"Was the news good?''

"Interesting—some movement of troops. There's no reason to suppose an invasion is imminent.''

"How did you get to London and back so quickly?''

"By horseback. Even at sixteen miles an hour in my curricle, there wasn't time. I've spent the better part of the day galloping, *ventre à terre*, to make it back before the assembly was over.''

"Why were you in such a hurry?'' she asked. Lord Dicaire didn't answer in words, but his smile was answer enough. "You must be very tired,'' she said in an unsteady voice.

"Not too tired to waltz. I want to hold you in my arms.''

When the music began, they waltzed, and when they remained together for a second dance, it was taken for confirmation by the watchers that Miss Judson had indeed nabbed herself a prime parti. Heads nodded wisely, but Mary Anne didn't see them. She didn't see anything but those dark eyes caressing her.

When the party was over, Lord Dicaire joined Lord Edwin, in the full expectation that he would be invited to spend the night at the Hall. He was not disappointed.

"I hope I can convince you to accept the hospitality of

Horton Hall for a few days, Dicaire," Lord Edwin said. He frowned and added, "A contradiction in terms, what? But you're welcome to a feather tick and Plummer's burned offerings."

"As I've already made up my bed, I shall accept," Lord Dicaire said blandly.

Fitch was late in coming. Half a dozen people offered them a ride home, but Lord Edwin waved them on.

"My groom will be here shortly." He smiled.

When the building was locked and deserted, they were still standing. "What has happened to Fitch?" Lord Edwin demanded a dozen times.

"Where did you see him last?" Lord Dicaire asked.

"I made the mistake of giving him three guineas when I got—that is, his salary, you know. I was a little in arrears."

Lord Dicaire was careful not to ask any more questions on that score. "The tavern, then," he said. "I'll fetch him."

He found Fitch lounging over a table, singing at the top of his lungs.

"Where's Lord Edwin's carriage, Fitch?" he asked.

"You're back for a dose of my home brewed?" Fitch asked, ready to hit somebody.

"No, your carriage. Where is it?"

"At home in the stable."

"You must have driven it to town. Think, where is it? At the inn?"

"Nay, I drove Joseph Horton's hay wain. You never looked at our hay wain. It was there all the time, right in plain sight, till I borrowed Jeremy's boat. But then the rain came, so I got it into the barn. It was a tough climb up to the loft, but easier bringing it down. Made it in one trip tonight—a hundred bales. I must take Joseph's hay wain

181

back before he misses it, and fetch the carriage. The old boy will turn rusty if I'm late."

Lord Dicaire thought for a moment, figuring out what had transpired. He could forgive Fitch's condition when he considered the amount of lifting and carrying he must have done the past few days. Taking the silk from the lugger to hide it in the old derelict hay wain, moving it to the boat, to the barn, to the hayloft, to Joseph's hay wain and thence, presumably, to the local draper. It was the most complicated feat of engineering since Hannibal had manuevered his elephants over the Alps.

Fitch deserved his rest, but how were they to get home? A smile lifted his lips. "Where's Joseph's hay wain?" he asked.

"Out back of the tavern."

"Sleep tight, Fitch," he said, and left.

It was a quarter of an hour before Lord Dicaire drove up to the assembly hall in the hay wain. "Climb aboard," he said.

"Eh? What's this?" Lord Edwin demanded. "Fitch! He's gone and drunk himself into a stupor. That's what it is. Ah, well, I've nothing against a hay ride. Give me a hand up, Mary Anne."

Lord Dicaire hopped down. "You're driving, Uncle," he said, and tossed him the reins.

Lord Edwin frowned. "Am I your uncle?" he asked.

"Not yet, but you will be when I marry your niece."

"Ah, you've arranged it with Peachie's son, then. Good work. I like a fellow who takes charge."

"We can't drive home in a hay wain!" Mary Anne exclaimed. She snickered to think of the elegant Lord Dicaire, sunk to such a shift.

"Too toplofty?" Dicaire teased, and tossed her up on what was left of the hay.

"Gee up, you old jades," Lord Edwin said, and the horses lurched forward into the night.

All was suspiciously quiet behind him, save for an occasional rustling in the hay.

Mary Anne lay on her back, looking up at the sky, which was spangled with tiny stars. Lord Dicaire lay beside her on his stomach, looking at the pale, enchanting oval of her face, and her dark eyes.

He plucked a straw from her hair. "I want to apologize for this morning, Mary Anne. When I suggested you set me free—I felt a perfect fool when you tore up at me. Rightly so! I had no idea how close you were to your uncle. Plummer told me a few things. That suggestion was only a desperate attempt to escape."

"I wanted to free you, James, but I couldn't. I just couldn't."

"I admire your faithfulness. I wouldn't give a brass farthing for a woman without it. I had known for days I loved you. That was the moment I knew I must marry you. Your uncle—and Peachie's son—capitulated easily. Now I must convince *you* to have me."

She gazed lovingly at him. Moonlight highlighted the shape of his brow, the slash of his nose, and cast the rest in shadows. She couldn't see him very well, but she felt the excitement of his closeness and felt his breath warm on her cheek.

"I can't imagine why you'd want to marry someone like me," she said with perfect honesty.

"That's one of the reasons. You have no idea how irresistible you are. Don't you ever look in a mirror?"

"All the time, but—"

"Well, you aren't in love with yourself, so perhaps you don't see what I see."

"I'm afraid I lack town polish, James."

He touched the curve of her cheek, which glowed in the

183

moonlight. "Any gem may be polished. It is the quality that interests me," he murmured. "I've wanted to do this ever since I saw you at the inn," he said, and pulled her into his arms to kiss her.

The kiss blended perfectly with the night and the stars. It was like another gift of nature. The first strangeness soon passed, and she felt at ease in his arms, despite the excitement that raced in her blood. No thought of the thousands of acres of his estate or of the London mansion occurred to her. She only knew she had magically found the man who was made for her, and she reveled in his love.

After an ardent embrace, he lifted his head. "Well? You haven't told me your feelings, Mary Anne."

"I think you already know them. My diary . . ."

"Good lord, I didn't read that!" he exclaimed. "Er, what did it say?"

"It said 'Tonight at the inn I met the sort of gentleman I should like to marry.' I was so embarrassed to think you had read it, and here am I, telling you!"

"I look forward to hearing what else you wrote," he said, and pulled her into his arms again.

As Lord Edwin jiggled the reins, it occurred to him that he had done a pretty good week's work. No need to squander any blunt on a trousseau, after all. Dicaire liked to handle things for himself. He could get a carriage to go with the new team. He'd make his maiden voyage to—now where the devil was it that Dicaire lived? He'd need a new jacket to go visiting noblemen. Already owed the tailor fifty or sixty pounds. He could pay, say, ten on account. By jingo, Dicaire might put in a word for him at Whitehall about his pension! One hand left the reins and began tapping his check thoughtfully.